Rob stood up; I did likewise. I couldn't tell if he was planning to end the conversation or not. We held each other's gaze for a long time. At first his eyes were angry, then they softened.

"Like I said, let me know when you and Jared call it quits."

"If you had stayed around long enough the other night, you'd have found out that Jared had a date with Carmen!" I paused to let that soak in. "Jared is a good friend of mine, and I intend to keep it that way. He's like the brother I never had."

"*Brothers* in that sense frequently turn out to be something more," he said coolly.

I didn't respond but thought of the summer morning Jared had kissed me and told me how he felt about me.

"Running into ex-boyfriends everytime I come around here could get a little odd."

"Jared is a *friend*," I repeated firmly.... Did he realize how inconsistent he sounded? Which was the real Rob? Did he want a girl whom he could persuade to drop an old friend for no reason? Or did he really want a girl with convictions and a mind of her own?

Boyfriends And Boy Friends

By Dianna Booher:

That Book's Not in Our Library
They're Playing Our Secret
Boyfriends and Boy Friends

Dianna Booher

Boyfriends And Boy Friends

FLEMING H. REVELL COMPANY
OLD TAPPAN, NEW JERSEY

Library of Congress Cataloging-in-Publication Data

Booher, Dianna Daniels.
Boyfriends and boy friends.

Summary: Despite the insistence of everyone around her that boys and girls cannot be ordinary friends, teenaged Leanne is determined to maintain her long-standing, non-romantic, friendship with the troubled Jared.
[1. Friendship—Fiction. 2. Assertiveness (Psychology)—Fiction. 3. High schools—Fiction. 4. Schools—Fiction. 5. Christian life—Fiction]
I. Title.
PZ7.B6449Bo 1988 [Fic] 87–28777
ISBN 0–8007–5274–0

Published by the Fleming H. Revell Company
Old Tappan, New Jersey 07675
Printed in the United States of America

Boyfriends And Boy Friends

chapter one

"Listen, Leanne, I won't see you at the game tomorrow night," Rob told me over the phone on Wednesday. "Dad and I are leaving early in the morning for M.I.T. Going to fly up and look over the campus one last time before I change my mind about next fall."

I tried to sift the disappointment from my voice. "Sounds like fun. Did you get an excused absence?"

"Timmons says there's no excuse for me." He let the words hang in the air, as if waiting for me to catch the double meaning. I did, but I didn't let him know it.

Instead, I said, "Well, don't forget to take along the newspaper story." The feature story the *Gazette* ran on him as Senior of the Month was fantastic; the picture made him look like a Greek god, bronzed muscles and all. They photographed him on the diving board with his look of deep concentration before taking the plunge. And the reporter had thrown in all the impressive details about the many tournaments Rob had won in the past four years. But in case an athletic scholarship somehow failed to materialize, the reporter went on to suggest, an academic one would likely be forthcoming. She also detailed some of Rob's accomplishments as student council president and, in general, painted him as the all-around best catch of the year.

"Yeah, I can just see me carting around five hundred copies and hawking them on every street corner in Boston, preparing them for Big Rob."

"No kidding," I said, "you should take a few copies. You can never tell when a little publicity might help, especially when a financial-aid committee starts putting their heads together about money."

"You're right. Maybe I'll take a thousand or two."

I grinned at his "humility" and turned my back to Mother, who had just come into the kitchen to get a drink of water. She drank all of two swallows. I could tell she was puzzled about who was on the other end of the line. She prides herself on our mother-daughter relationship. Sometimes I feel as though she's keeping a time card on our talks, as a measurement of how good a mother she is.

"Well, listen, I've got to hang up now," Rob said. "Spike is coming by, and we're going back to the gym to practice a few dives. Of course, *I* don't need the practice," he teased. "It's *his* three-and-a-half-somersault pike that's the pits."

"Just make sure they've got water in the pool," I deadpanned. He'd told me about being so nervous for his first tournament in ninth grade that he'd gotten up on the board before realizing he'd reported to the wrong YMCA pool.

"I'll call you on the weekend."

"Okay. Sounds great." I suppressed a squeal. Last Saturday night, I'd concluded that he was serious about dating me again. But I'm never really sure, even when a boy says that, that he really means it. Not that I've had that much experience dating. But I can name girlfriend after girlfriend who has gone over the intimate details of first dates and the promises of invitations to come, and then nothing ever materialized. And I've tried to help them sort out the conversations and events—to decide where they went wrong. Sheer agony.

Mother was still standing by the sink with her water glass in hand. I could feel her eyes on me.

"You did say you weren't dating anyone else?" Rob verified.

"No, of course not. Friday or Saturday night—either sounds great."

"Good. I'll see you in school, when I get back."

"Okay. Have fun."

I knew Mother would blanch at my giving Rob blanket notice that I was available at his convenience. Maybe that's why I hadn't told her much about our first date on Saturday night. This was going to be an out-of-the-ordinary relationship. Rob didn't play games, and he didn't expect me to. This wasn't the coquettish fifties Mother remembered. Rob and I had already found common ground. If you liked someone, why not let him know it? "No games" was how he'd put it on our first and only date.

I started out of the kitchen but didn't make it before seeing Mother arch her eyebrow in my direction. "Jared?"

"No. Rob."

I walked on out, and she didn't pursue the subject. Only in the privacy of my room did I dare give Rob's question more thought. *Was there someone else? Did Jared count?*

I contemplated the matter off and on until we began warming up for our away game at Brimble Thursday night. As the other high school in Herrington, Brimble was our most important rival. I hadn't seen Jared in almost two weeks. Rote basketball drills always allow you plenty of time for soul-searching, with no enemy colors leaping in between red-and-white warm-ups.

"He's still waiting. I think you ought to at least see what he wants," Tina said as she passed the ball on to the next player in line. Tina's my alter ego, prodding me on because I'm unassertive, as my mother says. I guess someone has to lead the innocents, right?

Just as I turned around to answer Tina, the basketball slapped me upside the head. My hand flew to my cheek to press the flesh to stop the sting. I felt like a marionette that had just had her head string jerked violently.

"Sorry. I thought you were looking," Kathi Ross screamed across the court at me.

I ignored her and held my cheek with both hands. The sting spread out like a cobweb across the whole side of my face. I knew I was flushed bright red, and I didn't dare glance up at the stands, to see who had been watching.

"Pay attention out there. Look alive," Coach Charba yelled at me.

Without glancing in her direction, I batted the ball away to Tina, who heaved it across the empty space to the next in line.

Tina whispered to me, "Kathi saw us talking; she knew you weren't expecting that pass. That was on purpose."

"Well, at least I know she didn't mistake me for the backboard." I continued to hold my face to stop the sting and watched the ball shoot from one player to the next down the line and back to me again.

"Aren't you going to say anything to her?" Tina prodded.

"No."

"I give up on you."

I shrugged at the pronouncement she'd made to me at least once a week ever since we had been best friends.

We kept the ball zipping down the row and back for a good two minutes before Coach blew the whistle to change drills.

Finally, Tina picked up with me again in mid-conversation. "Well, are you?"

"What do you expect me to say to her?"

"No, I mean, are you going outside to talk to Jared?"

"I can't." I glared at her, not believing she was still serious about me sneaking out. "You know I can't. When can I?"

"When Coach lets us go get a drink and go to the rest room. That's long enough. She won't miss you, then—everybody's scattered."

"Why can't he just come in and watch the game like everybody else? We can talk afterward." I was talking to myself as much as to Tina.

"You should know why he does the screwball things he does better than I do. He just said to tell you he wasn't coming inside the gym and for me to send you out. I didn't know what to tell him. I'm not your keeper. Charba was coming down the hall, anyway. What did you want me to tell him?"

"Figure eight," Coach Charba yelled in our direction.

We regrouped ourselves at both ends of the invisible eight and set the drill in motion. This drill left little time for conversation, and that suited me fine. I ran the figure eight automatically, dribbling and handing off without even realizing I'd touched the ball.

I kept wondering why Jared was outside. He knew I couldn't come out before the game without risking getting benched. And I knew that even if I took my chances and sneaked out and got away with it, talking to him wouldn't change anything. He'd only turn on the hurt puppy-dog look and make me feel guilty. After three years, Jared knew me well enough to know that it worked. I think that's probably part of what Mom and Tina call my unassertiveness—guilt.

I thought of Jared again, standing outside the gym in the midwinter Texas wind. Tina had said he looked bad. She's always a little dramatic, but still. . . . Jared had been especially depressed since school started. It seemed like every week into the semester got worse. But, of course, I couldn't blame him during the holidays. Having Thanksgiving and Christmas without his mother for the first time was rough. I'd hung around at his house at Christmas more than usual because I could tell everything about the decorations and the baking his grandmother did reminded him of things his mother had once done.

We tried not to think about it, but maybe that wasn't what he needed. Maybe I should have. . . . See? There I go again, blaming myself for how Jared felt. Don't get me wrong: I wanted to help him when he was feeling down, but sometimes I didn't think I was getting through. I suggested that he talk to his school counselor, but he reacted to that with the enthusiasm of facing a firing squad. Then I suggested he talk to Matt the Man, who hangs around our campus every day. But he said he didn't want to be preached to, and I couldn't convince him Matt wasn't like that. So what was I supposed to do, tie him up and drag him to a shrink?

Tina dribbled the ball into Melinda Pullen, Kathi Ross's best friend, and took her place in line behind us. Melinda gave her a drop-dead look and dribbled her way to the other end of the eight.

"You know I'll get caught." I continued to plead my case to Tina. "You *know* me. I'm chicken through and through. I can't even eat a butterscotch in history without looking guilty."

"You've got a point," Tina nodded, pulling at a hangnail for a moment. "But if anything happens, don't say I didn't tell you."

"If what happens?"

"I told you Jared wants to see you pretty bad. He just may . . . I don't know. He just looked bad—like he'd lost his last friend."

"He doesn't *have* any to lose," I mumbled to myself. But it was his own fault. He really had a lot to offer, when he wasn't so self-conscious.

I accepted the next dribble and rushed forward, batting the ball to the floor in smooth, angry spats. Why couldn't Jared snap out of it? Of course, I expected some moodiness. I loved his mother, too. Especially the last year, when Jared and I hung around his home pretty close in case she needed anything.

But six months was plenty of time to make friends at a new

school. After all, going to Brimble was his decision. I had helped Jared persuade his dad to let him drop out of private school and enroll at Brimble in the fall. Public schools weren't so bad, I told his dad. I was Exhibit A. His dad had winked and later given in. But Jared definitely was not making it in all the ways that counted with his dad.

Just as I got back to the figure eight, Coach Charba came toward us and started the rebound drill. She held the ball a minute, until the first few of us got in line, then tossed it toward the backboard. The first player bobbed up and batted the ball back. The second player batted the next ball. The third. The fourth, and so on.

Kathi lined up right in front of me and slammed her ball so hard against the board that it went over my head. So much for the rhythm of the pitter-pat. Tina was probably right: The earlier pass to my face had been no accident.

While I was bringing up the end of the line, the ten-minute warning sounded. Coach motioned for us to gather up the balls and come in, then go to the rest room and get a drink. Be back in eight minutes. She was always giving us odd time limits like that, so we'd take them seriously.

Against my better judgment, I walked past the line at the water fountain, straight out of the gym into the cold.

Standing with my back to the door, I squinted and searched the shadows for Jared. With a real chance to come out district high-point scorer for the season, I tried not to think about what being benched would do to me. Coach had once told my mother that I had more potential than any player she'd ever coached. After two more years of high-school ball, she had said I could name my scholarship.

That's another thing Rob and I have in common—a bird's-eye view of a scholarship.

Jared touched my arm; I swung around, startled. Then I

stepped back into the shadows, away from the doorway. "Hurry. I'm not supposed to be out here," I said.

"If you're in that big of a rush, you might as well go back in now."

Now he tells me? I just stared at him. He leaned back, propping himself against the wall, hands in his pockets. I waited, shivering, feeling the cold air evaporate the perspiration collected under my warm-up. The staredown didn't take long. Jared dropped his eyes to the inside of his jacket lapel, tugged at the zipper, hooked, and rehooked it.

Finally, I said, "Well, I've got to go back in, if you don't want anything."

"At least you came out here."

"What . . . are . . . you . . . talking . . . about?" I punctuated each word. "Will you say something? I mean, I'm not going to ask you why you won't come into the gym and watch the game. I'm sure you have a perfectly logical reason—like somebody might spit on you."

I was sorry I said that, as soon as it came out. But he was always putting himself down, and that gets to you after a while. He didn't used to do that so often. Just lately.

"I wanted to know if you still cared enough to come out here."

"Ask me after I get benched for the next game."

"Look, I'm sorry. I just want to know how you really feel, that's all."

"Jared, please. We've discussed all this—in a roundabout way, at least. I want us to still be friends. I just want to date others, too."

"But *I* don't want to date anybody else."

I didn't say anything.

"But I know *you* do." His eyes hung on me.

Silence.

"How did Saturday night with Rob go?" he asked after a minute.

"Okay." I avoided his eyes. Certainly, I wasn't going to tell him the whole truth in splendid detail. A year ago I could have told him, and he would have understood. He would have encouraged me and probably congratulated me. Now everything had changed. One kiss at the wrong time had wiped out three years of friendship and replaced it with—with what? I couldn't put the feelings into words, but the unnamed tension threatened our friendship.

When I looked at him again, I knew I should say something to make him feel better. But what could I say? Any nice thing I said, he'd take as encouragement, hoping that I didn't really mean it when I'd suggested he date someone else.

I tried changing the subject. "I like your jacket."

"You want to see it in burgundy or navy tomorrow? Maybe hunter green?"

"Your dad?"

He nodded. "I'm supposed to be keeping a list of where I wear what, so when he gets back, he can check out the results."

"Look, Jared, there are worse things to complain about. I mean, he's just trying to . . . well, maybe it's his way of showing. . . ."

"It's his way of saying I'm a dud of a son and let's see if he can buy a winner."

"Jared."

"Forget it."

He leaned back against the building, jammed his hands deeper in his pockets, and then propelled himself forward again with both feet on the ground. "I should have known from the beginning that you'd do this."

"Do what?"

"Break it off when we got serious."

I didn't have a clue as to what he was talking about. Break it off? We weren't even "together," in the sense he meant it. Oh, sure, we were together—riding horses and playing tennis in his backyard. But that wasn't exactly my idea of romance.

"I don't know what you're talking about," I said.

"My height, remember?"

"You know I was kidding." No way could he have taken me seriously about someone spitting on him.

He continued as if he hadn't heard me. "It's the pool and the horses, isn't it?"

"I can't believe this! I can't believe you're really standing there and. . . ."

"Forget it," he cut me off again. His voice caught in his throat. "I'm sorry."

"It's okay." The anger went out of my voice. I could see his tears glisten in the dim light shining through the small gymnasium door window. He ducked his head again, so I couldn't see his face.

"Jared, I'm really sorry, too. I just don't know how else to say it. I like you. I really like you a lot. For three years, you've been my best friend. Closer than Tina, even, because of what we've been through."

I stopped there because I didn't want to remind him of his mother's death. I'm still convinced that because of what happened then, things began to change between us. "It's just that I want to date other people." *Namely Rob,* I thought.

"Well, this is the last time I'm going to bother you. I really mean it. You won't be seeing me around. Anywhere."

I didn't say anything because when I'm not sure how to react, I try to wait it out. Jared had talked like this before the funeral, hinting that he was going to hurt himself. At first, it upset me. I could never tell if he was serious. Then I decided that it was mainly to get his dad's attention—something that was scarce, even when his mother was alive.

"Why don't you call up another friend? Go somewhere for the weekend?"

"Yeah. Sure. All one of them."

Maybe he didn't have many friends, but he brought it on himself by being so paranoid. He said no one liked him for what he was, but that wasn't true, especially in my case. Sure, I'd been impressed with his house, the servants, the riding stables and horses. But I certainly hadn't thrown myself at him, then or now. How serious could you get in seventh grade? Our fathers had introduced us at a company family picnic one weekend. Seventh grade seemed so long ago I hardly remembered it.

After a minute or two longer, Jared again propelled himself away from the wall with his foot, turned to face me, and brushed his brown hair to the side with his cupped fingers.

I looked at my watch again. Seven minutes.

"I mean it. I won't bother you anymore," he said, turning abruptly and heading for the parking lot. I watched as he sauntered along. He looked like someone's kid brother, not a boyfriend. He'd borrowed his dad's Mercedes again, which he'd been doing since eighth grade, when he didn't have a license. Did that mean his dad was out of town again? That Jared was going to be home alone?

I shuddered, either from the cold or the clammy perspiration or from my thoughts. *I'd done all I possibly could, hadn't I? I couldn't be responsible forever, could I?*

chapter two

Mother pulled in to the lot beside the bus and waited while we drearily climbed off about midnight. It was cold, especially for Texas in midwinter, and I shivered as I left the warmth of the bus and piled into our car. Across the lot, I could see the school stretching out in the darkness, like a tall, sleeping giant. A few lights illuminated the doors and bounced off some windows, but overall, the school looked tired and lonely.

"Don't coaches know this is too late for a school-night game?"

"They *give* the exams—they don't *take* them."

She started the engine, backed up, and maneuvered out of the slot. Then she suddenly slammed on the brakes when Melinda and Kathi hit the back of our car with their duffel bags. Giggling, they came around to Mother's window as she lowered it and stuck her head out.

"I almost hit you girls," she said, her voice still shaky.

They laughed. "Yeah, well. Sorry. But would you just back up and shine your car lights down there?" Melinda asked, pointing to the pavement behind our taillights.

"What for?"

Kathi let out a loud burp. "I lost my contact. Just shine them a minute." Still giggling, she pushed Melinda back around the rear of the car. Mother carefully turned the car around and shined the headlights on them.

They got down on all fours and started feeling the pavement in the stream of light. About the time I got out and offered to help them look, they got up. "Never mind. Never mind. I found it."

"She found it," Melinda echoed her friend.

"We found it, everybody!" They began howling into the wind as they wandered off toward Melinda's car. "Found a peanut, found a peanut, found a peanut just now. . . ."

I got back into the car, hoping they'd make it home. Mother backed up again, and we pulled out of the school lot.

"Sounds like they just wandered out of some bar," Mother commented.

"Yeah, backseat bar."

She asked me what I meant, and I told her that I thought they'd added something to their Coke cups on the bus. But I made a point to emphasize that it was no big deal. Practically half the student body drank at school functions, anyway. No big deal, I kept saying, hoping she would drop it. I mean, it's one thing for me to defend my decision when someone asks why I don't drink, but who wants her parents getting into it and getting other kids in trouble?

"Don't they have any training rules against that?"

"Girls like Kathi Ross never get caught."

My stomach felt queasy as I took a seat in the outer lobby of the principal's office and waited. Is this how other kids felt when I, as an office aide, traipsed in with similar notes for them during fourth period? I was sure the summons to the principal's office was about sneaking out before the game. But why the office? Coach Charba usually just gave us her lectures in the gym during workouts.

If I sound like an old pro about benching, I'm not. The only time I can remember anybody being benched was last year, when Hettie Silverton and Marta LaHayes missed a game without telling Coach ahead of time. Their excuse was some big weekend party at their boyfriends' college. So you can see benching is definitely not a frequently sought-after status symbol around here. For the most part, we're serious about winning. And Tina is right: I don't have the stomach for problems.

The secretary had her back to me and the principal's closed door. She typed first one form and then another in rapid succession, yanking them out of the typewriter as if she were the one about to get D-hall.

After a few minutes, I thought maybe there'd been a mix-up about the messages, so I cleared my throat. She didn't turn around to see what I wanted. Unlike Ms. Welsh in the attendance office, she never paid students any attention until you forced her to, and then she always acted like you'd interrupted her in the middle of signing a Middle East peace pact.

Finally, I took my chances and asked, "Mr. Timmons did want to see me, didn't he?"

"Yes, he did." She spat her words at me and yanked out another form. "He has two other girls in there now, and the coach. He said you should wait out here."

I nodded and settled back in my chair for a long winter. I could just see this spreading all over the school. But who would care? Sneaking out before a ballgame for a lousy seven minutes? What could you do in seven minutes, right? I couldn't help but shake my head; I had known all along that I'd get caught. I had tried to tell Tina that from the very beginning.

Just then, Rob walked through the lobby. "Hey, what are you doing down here?" he asked, coming my way.

"What are *you* doing here?" I countered, stalling to think of an explanation without having to mention Jared. "It is the middle of first period, you know? And when did you get back in town?"

"Last night. And I'm leaving again."

"For what?"

"That math tournament's today. Remember, I told you Saturday night?"

"Oh, yeah. Two absences in a row will plow you under in homework, won't it?"

"I'm afraid to ask for my assignments. I'll just take the big blow when I get back, all at once."

"Well, how do you feel?" As long as I could keep him talking about himself, I hoped we wouldn't get to me. But I didn't want to be too bubbly and too obvious. I reached into my pocket for a butterscotch out of habit, then remembered where I was.

"I always feel lucky. The Midas Touch." He curled his fingers then stretched them out toward me in spastic fashion.

Before I could come up with an excuse for sitting in front of the principal's office, he added, "I hear some of your teammies really had a good time last night on the bus back from Brimble."

"What do you mean?"

"The booze."

"Did they get caught? I didn't hear that."

"Somebody told me they're going to be suspended."

"Who?"

"I don't know who was involved," Rob elaborated. "I just heard Bojo mention it in the hall, congratulating somebody on a free holiday."

"Sounds like Bojo."

There was a silence. "Say, are you going to make me guess?" he asked.

"About what?" I was still stalling.

"What you're down here for?"

"Oh. Well, I think I'm in trouble with the coach, but she usually lets us have it in P.E. I don't know if that's why they called me down or not. I just got a note."

"Just a minute. I've got to see if Mr. Schroeder is waiting. I was supposed to meet him down here." Rob walked to the end of the lobby and pushed the door open to check the hallway for his math tournament sponsor.

I should have been more specific the first time I answered Rob. That's one of the reasons Mother is forever telling me to open up and tell people what's going on in my head. I'd feel pushy doing that, but she says you've got to look out for yourself, because nobody else is going to. My mother should have a long talk with Jared, right?

I certainly couldn't tell Rob that I was in trouble for sneaking out of the gym to see Jared. Not after Saturday night's discussion.

Although we'd covered about every subject in the book—math tournaments, scholarships, basketball, diving, politics, parents, and God—past boyfriends and girlfriends were the touchiest subjects. He'd mentioned that when he started dating a girl, he didn't want to waste his time getting to know her, if she was interested in someone else. Not that he dated that many girls. I never saw him with any *one* girl, really; it was closer to ten. His statement about not wasting his time getting to know someone sounded odd at first, but then I could see his point.

Intimacy on the intellectual and emotional level, Rob said, was really the missing ingredient in most teen relationships. Rob said he didn't like to ask girls out impulsively. He tried to be around them a while first, to see if he thought they'd really click.

It seemed almost like deciding to go steady before the first date. At first, I thought he was being arrogant. But from the look on his face, I could tell he was just being practical. He was too busy to waste time.

Rob took his student council job seriously. He even volunteered us to help in a community drive for used toys, clothes, and household goods for families hit by a tornado in a little town nearby. I would never have thought of that.

In addition to the usual council projects Rob was obligated to, this year he had to break in a new principal, and that took a little extra time. So you can see why he made a big deal about being sure from the start that I wasn't dating anyone else.

I saw his point, and I wasn't offended. My mother would have been.

"So what did you do that brought down the wrath of Charba the Barber?" Rob asked after he'd checked around the corner for Mr. Schroeder. "I didn't know she could get mad at star players."

I just raised my eyebrows at this last assumption. "She just has some strict rules. She wants us to think basketball twenty-four hours a day, at least."

"So—can she read your mind?"

I grinned. "I went outside the gym before the game at Brimble." I tried to say it offhandedly.

"You went outside the gym?" He lifted the corner of his mouth in that oh-yeah smile. "So what's the big deal?"

"She'd just issued an edict that we can't be talking to boyfriends or whoever after we start warm-ups. She doesn't want us out of her sight. Total absorption, you know?"

"Ahhh," he shook his head mockingly. "Who did you go out to see?"

"I . . . well, it wasn't my idea, really."

His grin faded, replaced by an absolutely blank expression.

"Tina kept telling me this friend of mine, Jared, wanted to talk to me."

"Who's Jared?"

"Just a friend."

"Since when?"

"Since seventh grade."

He didn't say anything.

I added, "He goes to Brimble. You don't know him."

"And you always do everything Tina tells you to do?"

"Well, she said he looked pretty upset." I wanted to tell him that Jared had been crying and was terribly depressed, but I couldn't do that to Jared.

"Well, I hope you made him all better." Rob looked down at his shoes, crossed his legs at the ankles, and propped himself against the wall with an elbow. After a moment, he said, "Look, like I said Saturday night, I don't want to interfere. If you're still going with Jared. . . ."

"I never was *going* with Jared. We're friends, that's all. We ride horses and swim. Our fathers know each other. His mother died this summer from cancer." I disliked bringing Mrs. Sahol into it; it seemed disrespectful after I'd said it. "We're friends, Jared and I, that's all."

Rob nodded and focused his big blue eyes on me, as if searching for the truth. I wished my feelings about Jared were as black and white as I'd just made them sound.

He stood propped on his elbow for a moment longer, saying nothing. Then finally, "Well, I've got to go. Schroeder must be having trouble finding his way out of his room."

I laughed. "He's the best they could do for a sponsor?"

"Grim, isn't it? Higher math escapes him, and he's trying to get me a scholarship?"

"Well, good luck."

"Yeah, thanks." He started to walk off, then paused. "I'd like to meet this friend Jared sometime. Okay?"

"Oh. Okay. Sure."

I watched him as he sauntered off, but he didn't look back. Then before he got out of earshot, I called after him, "Remember—just mark the little black dots."

"Got it. 'Blacken the entire space, filling each circle completely. When you have finished, close the test booklet with your answer sheet inside.' "

I could hear him continue to mumble the monotone on down the hallway. Had we really taken so many of those achievement tests since kindergarten that he had all the instructions memorized?

The secretary yanked another form out of the typewriter and threw another perturbed glare in my direction. Her face looked as sour as my stomach felt.

chapter three

Mr. Timmons's office door opened, and Melinda and Kathi walked out. Melinda had been crying. They gave me a look that would wither an oak just as Mr. Timmons appeared in the doorway and motioned for me. *So what had I ever done to them?*

The only place to sit was directly in front of Mr. Timmons's all-but-empty desk. The classroom teachers have desks about the size of orange crates to hold piles of papers; you could land an airplane on a principal's desk. Clout, my mother says. Being a professor at Belton University, she always fills me in on the quirks of the educational system.

Coach Charba didn't look in my direction but rather walked around behind my chair. I could feel her eyes on the back of my head.

Mr. Timmons, who resembled a mouse with wide ears and small mouth, finally glanced up. Generally, he was friendly with the students; unlike some of the vice-principals, he didn't treat students like part of the furniture.

"I guess you must know why we called you in," he said after a dramatically long pause.

"Yes . . . I guess."

"Well, what do you have to say?" he pulled at his ear.

"I'm sorry. I shouldn't have gone out."

With a surprised look, he glanced over my shoulder at Coach Charba.

I continued, "But can I at least tell you why?"

"Please do," he said with a little edge to his voice.

"Well, this boy that I like—a friend of mine—Jared Sahol, wanted to talk to me, and I was afraid that if I didn't go out and see what he wanted, he'd. . . . This sounds silly, but he gets depressed really easy and . . ." I paused, not knowing if I were giving too many details but wanting to give enough so they'd believe me. I finished, ". . . he thinks nobody likes him, and he wanted to talk to me. That's all."

"Leanne, you know what the rules are about that," Coach Charba spoke from behind me. "We play ball to win. Keeping your head in the game is hard enough, without having you sneak around taking care of boyfriend problems before game time."

"He's *not* my boyfriend."

"Well, whoever."

"In light of the rest of the evening," Mr. Timmons interjected, "I guess that was a minor offense."

"The rest of the evening? I don't know what you're talking about."

"Surely, you've heard about the little party the girls had on board the bus last night?"

"I was sitting up toward the front of the bus. Or in the middle, at least."

"Melinda and Kathi were just in here. They've admitted it."

I was relieved.

"They said they brought the orange juice and you supplied the vodka."

"I *what?*" My mouth fell open. I hoped they didn't think this was some kind of act, because I was floored.

Mr. Timmons stared at me with his lips pursed into an even smaller than usual circle. He waited.

"They're lying. Where would I get any vodka?"

"You just told us you left the gym before game time," Coach answered. I was getting it in stereo now.

"And I told you why," I tried to say evenly. I could feel my eyes starting to fill up; I can't help crying when I get angry. My ears burned, and I opened my eyes wider, trying to will myself to hold things in check.

"I went out to talk to Jared. Seven minutes. I wasn't even out there seven minutes. And that was *before* the game."

"I know when it was. I saw you." The stereo effect again. Then Coach Charba walked over to one side of the room, so I could see her out of the corner of my eye. "That was poor judgment on my part," she continued. "I should have benched you immediately, instead of waiting until this morning. If it had been any other team . . .," her voice trailed off.

"Really, Coach. Mr. Timmons," I looked at them both, trying to control my voice and make it flat, not a whine. "I didn't know for sure they had anything on the bus, and I certainly didn't get it for them. I can't believe this."

Neither of them answered.

"I've never been in trouble before." I'd been sent out in the hall for talking in second grade, but I didn't think that would count. "You *know* me," I pleaded with Mr. Timmons.

"Yes, I do. You've been very cooperative as an office aide. That's why this bothers me. I suspended the other two girls just now."

"Suspended?"

"That's school policy. Drinking on school property or at school functions—five days."

I waited for what seemed like another hour: Then, because he didn't say anything else, I repeated myself. "I *didn't* get them the vodka. Really. I just went out to talk to Jared. You can ask him."

"We will. Does he go to school here?"

"No. Brimble High."

"You can go back to class now. We'll send for you a little later, when we decide what to do." Mr. Timmons's eyes bored through me, then flickered relentingly. "I sure hope you're telling it straight—for your sake."

I started to say something else about how it would have been impossible for me to conceal a bottle until after the game, but decided against it.

I walked out of the office and back to class like a zombie. My first thought was to sneak down to the cafeteria and try to phone Jared at Brimble, so he would expect Mr. Timmons's call. But I vetoed the idea because they'd think I was telling him to lie for me. No, it'd be better if they surprised him. Surely the shock in his voice when he was called to the office to talk to the principal of another school would convince them we hadn't masterminded the Great Vodka Caper.

My eyes started to water again, and my ears stopped up. They assumed I was guilty until proven innocent! Maybe government wasn't a required course when Mr. Timmons attended high school.

First-period class lumbered on. I took my seat and stared straight ahead. *Suspension.* A chill went over me, and I tried to shake it off. Zeros in all my courses for five days. Even with a good solid *B* average, that many zeros would do me in for the six weeks, maybe the whole semester. Then it hit me like a ton of bricks; Wednesday started six-weeks' exams. I'd have to take a zero in any exam given Wednesday through Friday. What timing!

The bell to end the period sounded like something far, far away. Almost everybody was already out the door before I pulled myself together and moved out of my seat. I headed down the hall for second period as if in a soundproof bubble. I tried to visualize Jared being called to the phone, to hear him talking to

Mr. Timmons about why I'd been outside the gym. I didn't care if he convinced him we were passionate lovers who couldn't bear to be separated for the length of a basketball game—anything to persuade them I was telling the truth.

Earl the Squirrel bumped into me. I gave him a tight-lipped, stingy smile and moved on before he caught up with me. Despite my conscious effort to keep Melinda and Kathi off my mind, they forged to the front. I had always been a little afraid of them—Kathi, in particular. Afraid of what she was capable of doing. But I didn't want to think about them right there in the middle of the hall, because, like I said, when I get uncontrollably angry, I cry. And I certainly didn't want to hand them that little pleasure.

"Did you hear what happened?" Tina asked me as she put her books down beside me in second period. "Melinda and Kathi got suspended for five days. They're going to be out during exams."

"Maybe me, too."

Tina's eyes bugged out, and her forehead wrinkled in the usual lines. "What? For leaving the gym? That's crazy!"

"Melinda and Kathi told Mr. Timmons and Coach that I brought them the vodka and was drinking with them."

"You're kidding? I mean, I wouldn't put it past Kathi to try, but they can't just say something like that without proof."

"They did."

"Timmons didn't believe them, did he?"

I told Tina everything: about being called to the office, about seeing Rob, about Timmons calling Jared.

"What's Melinda and Kathi's main pain? The basketball upside the head, now this. Why you, and why now?"

"Kathi still likes Rob, for one thing."

"But they broke up last year. If you could say they were ever really going together."

"She can still like him, can't she?"

"But how did she know he took you out Saturday night?"

"How does she know everything else?"

"I can't believe they told Timmons an out-and-out lie."

"Believe it."

"Timmons'll get to the bottom of it. He always does," Tina tried to reassure me.

I thought it over and felt a little better. He did have a reputation for being competent and fair. He walks the halls, attends the ballgames, buys banquet tickets. He had okayed Matt, our youth minister, to hang around school. Surely, he had a heart somewhere in that little mouse body of his, didn't he?

Mrs. Wolenhueter began calling roll from the grade book again. She's another one of the disorganized, who never gets around to making a seating chart until second semester.

I leaned over to Tina. "At least Rob's out of the building today. He went to a math tournament."

"That's good."

"Otherwise, we might be finished as a twosome before we get started." She looked puzzled, but I didn't have time to explain about our previous conversation.

Mrs. Wolenhueter droned on, "Harbin, Jill. Hargraves, Bart. Harrell, Mike. Johnson, Beth. Johnson, Luke."

"Did you tell Mr. Timmons that Kathi was trying to get you in trouble? That she doesn't like you?" Tina whispered.

"No."

"Why not?"

"You can't say something like that."

"Why not?"

"Because it sounds juvenile."

"Does not. You never stand up for yourself. You've got to stand up for yourself."

"Yes, Mo-therrrr," I smirked.

"Well, suspension isn't exactly going to be a Broadway play. You know, your mother's right about you."

I merely glared at her. Just because I didn't pitch a screaming fit and give somebody a karate chop didn't mean I was a

Pollyanna or a pushover. Or did it? I preferred to have faith that things would work out, that intelligence beats hysteria.

I looked at Tina for a moment out of the corner of my eye, head straight toward Mrs. Wolenhueter, listening for Markwardt. After I answered "Present," I thought about Tina and my mother and how alike they were. Maybe there was some psychological reason she and I had become best friends.

But to tell Mr. Timmons about the conflict with Kathi *was* juvenile, no matter what Tina thought. Why should he care that Kathi suddenly didn't like me? It was not that we didn't get along, really. I just stayed out of her way, something that was rather difficult to do, since we played on the same basketball team. But she was second string, and that lessened the times our paths crossed. They didn't follow the same rules—and I'm not talking about basketball—as everybody else did. Kathi had no rules whatsoever; Melinda was her puppet.

Who knows? Maybe Mr. Timmons was afraid of her too. Last semester, after she'd made the drill team, Kathi had thrown a real fuss about the hair code, which she knew about before auditioning. The drill-team sponsor had drawn up a policy, part of which was that girls could wear their hair no longer than two inches below shoulder length. It was a matter of conformity. Everybody had accepted it.

At least until Kathi came along, they had. After she got on the drill team, she got up a petition saying that having to cut her goldie locks was discrimination, that she intended to be a model, and she needed her long hair. Eventually, she got enough signatures to get her way. I think most of them signed because she intimidated them. She came on strong about her dad, a lawyer, who thought students had their rights violated practically every day of the week and Kathi was the golden goddess who was going to rescue them.

She got her way. The school board asked that the drill-squad hair code be lifted. The drill-squad instructor quit.

Roll call ended. Mrs. Wolenhueter opened her book to the short story we were supposed to have read overnight. Just as she asked the first question about point of view, the intercom clicked on. Announcements. She always forgot to wait for them and then acted irritated at the unexpected interruption.

I tuned out Rob's replacement. The announcer had a high-pitched voice and whistled as he talked.

How could I prove the truth? Practically everybody on the bus had Styrofoam cups on the trip home last night. Who could say for sure who was drinking what? It was my word against theirs.

And why me? What did I ever do to cause them to spew their venom in my direction? Nothing, except have Rob show a slight interest in me. Which would probably fade immediately, if I didn't decide what to do about Jared.

That afternoon when I turned the corner of the almost-empty hallway in my usual rush to drop off my books and get to gym class before the tardy bell, Kathi and Melinda were standing near my locker. My pace quickened instinctively. They had their backs to me and evidently hadn't heard my footsteps on the carpet. Why weren't they in their next class, instead of hanging around my locker?

The faster I walked, the more panicky I felt. During the ten seconds it took me to walk down the hall toward my locker, I thought of how my mother would handle the situation. She would, in her strong alto voice dripping with sarcasm, ask if they had "some problem" she could help them with, knowing they would be intimidated and slink away without carrying out whatever they intended to do. I thought about my mother telling me I had to stand up for my own rights because nobody else was going to.

Kathi was jiggling my locker's handle when Melinda turned around and saw me behind them.

"What are you doing? That's my locker." I was surprised to hear my words had a firm, halfway threatening tone. Kathi turned around slowly, shook her long blond hair back, and cocked her chin in the air. Melinda, with the cold, empty stare she usually wore, stood shoulder to shoulder with her.

"Wrong locker, I guess," Kathi said, with a wouldn't-you-like-a-straight-answer smile.

They turned and hurried down the west wing.

I jiggled the combination lock. It was open. What had they been planning to get out of there? Or put in? I opened the door, shoved my books in, and moved things around. Nothing missing, nothing extra. I swirled the combination dial a couple of extra times and headed down to gym.

So what else was there to do about it?

At sixth-period gym, the note finally came. I was to report to the office immediately.

chapter four

Even though the open door rattled against the wall when I knocked, Mr. Timmons didn't look up. Teachers always want you to know they're very busy and when they give you their undivided attention, you had better make it quick. Mother even carries the behavior over at home, and before Dad moved out, it used to drive him crazy. Finally, he got to the point where he never told her anything. I figure that's why she makes such a point now to more or less schedule our discussions of the day's trivia during mealtime.

Mr. Timmons finished what he was writing, pushed the papers into one neat stack, and finally made eye contact.

"Sit down."

I backed into the chair and held my breath.

"We talked to your boyfriend, Jared." He paused, seeming to prolong the suspense on purpose.

"He's not my boyfriend."

"Whatever," he smiled in a paternal, amused way before continuing. "And he told the same story you did. He insisted there was no way you could have gotten any vodka in the length of time you came out to talk to him." He rubbed one of his mouselike ears a moment longer.

"I honestly didn't have anything to do with it, Mr. Timmons. I didn't."

He continued to press his ear between his thumb and forefinger and then pulled it taut from his head, like an Ace bandage.

"We don't like to falsely accuse students. You know that," he paused, as if waiting for me to nod agreement. I did. "That's the reason I've spent a good deal of my day getting to the bottom of this. I talked to both Melinda and Kathi again before they went home. Talked to them separately this time. And there were some discrepancies in their stories about your part in their little escapade."

I swallowed noisily, feeling as though I could breathe again. I knew the system wouldn't let me down. I'd always played by the rules—always—except this once. My uncle, a principal at a junior high in another district, says that's what every kid at his school claims whenever they get caught. Still, seven minutes outside before a ballgame is not exactly what you'd call juvenile delinquency.

"But our main . . ." Mr. Timmons took his time searching for the right word, ". . . reason for believing you—aside from the fact that everything Jared said checked out and aside from the discrepancies in the other two girls' stories—is that I think it would be highly unlikely that your mother would have reported the incident if you had been involved."

"My *mother*?" The bottom fell out of my stomach as though I were on a long elevator descent. Just wait until Kathi got a hold of that news. "My mother?" I repeated, hoping I'd misunderstood.

He nodded. "She was the one who phoned Coach Charba last night and told her about the drinking on the bus."

When I didn't speak, he continued, "And we don't think that if you had been tipsy when you got home, your mother would have phoned to report the others and chance your getting in trouble, too."

"Yeah. Well . . . uh . . . I didn't know she called."

"Obviously."

"I didn't tell her to. Look, my mother just saw and heard them when Kathi lost her contact. . . ."

"Well, I wouldn't be too hard on your mother. School policy is no good unless it can be enforced. I only wish we had a few more parents who cared enough to report situations like this."

Silence from me.

"But I do want to warn you, Leanne, about leaving the Brimble gym and breaking any other rules Coach Charba has set up." He paused to let the silence grow. "Teachers around here are far less respected than we'd like, and this administration is determined to do something about it." He patted the stack of papers on his desk rather firmly, but his voice softened. "Now I know sneaking out of a gym doesn't seem like a major offense, but she has her reasons, I'm sure. I think she's going to discuss that with you later."

I nodded. I could wait for that. Benching would nix my chances as district high-point, for sure.

He plucked at the corners of his mouse ears once more, and then stood up. I followed his lead.

"Now I don't want to see you in my office again for something like this. You're not that kind of student. Ms. Welsh, in the attendance office, says you're a dependable aide."

I gradually backed out of the doorway, then rounded the corner and picked up my pace.

My own mother! I locked my jaws, yanked my books out of my locker, and accidentally slammed the door on my fingers. Just one more high point of the day. The halls had cleared, which was a good thing, in my frame of mind. We never had workouts on

Fridays, so Coach Charba would just have to wait until Monday to tell me about the benching.

Outside the building, the cold wind hit me in the face, but I hardly felt it. No wonder Kathi had lied about me giving them the vodka; she must have found out that it was my mother who reported them! Well, it was her own fault, sticking her head in the window and breathing all over Mother and giggling like a moron.

Or maybe Rob told Kathi. After all, he knew before he left for the math tournament that somebody was getting suspended. But that was crazy; he had no way of knowing Mother had phoned. My mind whirred as wildly as a pinball machine.

I stepped off the curb on the side of my foot; a sharp pain pierced my ankle, which then began to throb like my smashed fingers. Slowing down, I glanced at my watch; I could really cover territory when angry. Wonder if it would work on the basketball court?

As soon as the receptionist saw me walk into the English Department at Belton U, she reported that mother had gone to the snack bar to get a Tab. Did I want to have a seat and wait? *Did I have a choice?*

I spoke to the two graduate students posing as typists in the front office: Geraldine, a newlywed who was Mother's most dependable help, and Marta, who worked only enough to pay next month's rent. I reminded myself that a good-paying job for the next two summers might spare me from crowding my college schedule with such boredom.

Cloistering myself in the cubbyhole my mother called an office, I waited. The picture of me from eighth grade was still sitting on her desk. Such a silly smile. It looked like the photographer had caught me in the middle of a yell. Mother liked the picture, insisting that it was my most normal pose.

In the top drawer were some butterscotches, which I unwrapped and popped in my mouth. All her makeup was neatly arranged in open cardboard boxes in the drawer. She keeps a supply at the office for the times Philip picks her up directly from work and for the days she's working practically around the clock to publish a journal article. Her job would be a breeze, she always said, if teaching were all there was to it.

A list of all the teaching assistants and the classes they taught lay in the center of her desk. Obviously, she was still working on organizing them into a walkout for more wages. Slave labor, she called it. The TAs working with the full professors usually found themselves grading papers, a chore not too appealing to students who thought they were the intelligentsia of modern society. And their menial, boring tasks were performed for a pittance. Unless she gets fired first, my mother, as the only member of the administration sympathetic to the TA cause, will change things.

She walked in.

I looked her straight in the eye. "Why did you do it?"

"Do what?" She avoided my eyes and picked up a publisher's catalog out of the chair, marking her place before closing it.

"You know what I mean. Calling the coach."

She posed, as if contemplating the question, then looked away again. "Somebody had to. Might as well have been me. I should have mentioned it to you, I guess."

"You *guess*? Do you know what they'll do to me?"

"Who?"

"Melinda and Kathi."

"I didn't give any names to the coach."

"That doesn't make any difference. They found out who easily enough."

"How?"

"How should I know? Kathi knows everything, almost before it happens."

"I don't know what they can do to you. You didn't have anything to do with it, anyway. I'll take full responsibility for reporting the incident."

"Motherrrr!" I screeched. Surely she wasn't that naive.

"Sins of the fathers, is that it?"

I wasn't sure if she'd meant her question to be a dig at my new faith, but now wasn't the time to get into that. Let's just say she didn't share or encourage my beliefs.

"Do you know what they already did to me?" I pushed the point further.

She finished clearing a place for me to sit on the desk, but I ignored her offer and stood. I have little enough backbone standing, much less sitting.

"They almost got me suspended, that's all."

"How could *they* get *you* suspended?"

"They said I gave them the vodka."

She smiled sardonically.

"I don't see what's funny."

"Sorry. Nothing's funny. It's just that no one would say that if they knew what we'd been through."

"But they don't, and that's the point."

We'd had Grandmother in and out of hospitals for alcoholism and its effects until she had died two years ago. Mine were religious convictions; Mother's were from purely practical experience. I could understand why she felt like she did about alcohol, but she was missing the whole point about the school affair.

"I almost got five days' suspension. I would have missed exams and maybe failed the whole semester because of it."

"Don't be dramatic. You're sounding like Tina."

"Mother, do you hear me? You almost got me suspended!"

"I said I'm sorry. But I take it from your verb tense that this is a past worry. You used your mouth, told them the truth, and stood up for yourself?"

"Yes, I did. I sure did. All they had to do was call Jared to verify my story." I told her all the details about sneaking out of the gym to talk to Jared and the impending benching. But she seemed more pleased than upset—pleased that I'd done what I thought was best about going out to talk to him and thought for myself.

It really was a twist, my relationship with my mother. To her, rules and policies are always negotiable, and working to change the system adds spice to her life. She can't understand why I don't have what it takes to take matters that need changing into my own hands.

She stood up again, walked around her desk, and put her arms around my shoulders from behind me. "I'm sorry, honey. I only did what I thought was right. In the first place, they have no right to be drinking on the bus; they know it's against school policy. And besides that, they're hurting the whole team's performance. You should care about that—you're part of that."

I didn't answer. It was not that I didn't agree with her in principle; I just couldn't forget the repercussions for me.

"And that's not to mention their driving home drunk. They're just lucky both of them weren't killed, if Melinda was driving."

I didn't tell her that was exactly how they got home.

"You've still got to learn to be assertive, to take up for yourself," she added.

"I did."

"Good."

End of subject. She retrieved the publisher's catalog and thumbed through it. I couldn't see her face through the cascade of auburn hair swinging forward.

She would never understand that I'm a different person from her, that I can't be as assertive as she is. After attending one of those assertiveness seminars, she had come home saying it was all just common-sense material that she already knew. And she was right; my mother had always been able to stand up for herself. When she and Dad had worked out the divorce settlement, he claimed that she had "cleaned his plow."

But at least the bitterness between them is gone now. It's been four years. My dad even comes in to chat sometimes when he picks me up for the weekend, which isn't too often, since he travels.

But I'm just not like her, and she knows all too well my tendency to let things work themselves out. Melinda and Kathi wouldn't let this go, I knew, and my mother would never understand why I couldn't handle it and stand up to them.

"Are you and Rob going out this weekend?" she asked after a moment.

"I don't think so."

"You don't *think* so?" She cocked an eyebrow at me.

"No. We're not."

"I thought he asked you on the phone the other night."

"He just mentioned that we might get together. Nothing definite. I guess something came up."

I didn't believe that something came up any more than she did. But he definitely hadn't mentioned us going out again.

"Some*thing*, or some*one*?"

"What do you mean?"

"Like Jared? I hope you're not letting Jared stand in the way of a new relationship, if it's what you want." She got up out of the chair and sat down again on the edge of her desk.

I didn't respond, so she continued, "I hope you're not going to try to ride the fence here. I don't think a guy like Rob—from what you've told me—will play second fiddle to anybody else."

"I didn't ask him to."

"Listen. Is Jared still trying to dump his problems on you?"

"We're friends, that's all."

"Friendship has its limits, Leanne. That boy is too much a loner. Maybe he needs more help than you can give him."

"It's his dad who needs the help," I mumbled.

"In what way?"

"I don't know. He's always putting Jared down. And he's drunk most of the time. Acts like he's sixteen again, but he's practically middle-aged. I don't know—he just acts weird since Mrs. Sahol died."

"What do you mean weird?"

"Never mind. I don't know. Forget it."

She held her gaze on me for a long time, but I didn't know how to answer. I regretted having told her as much as I did about my conversation with Rob Saturday night. Late at night, I always feel talkative; the next morning, vulnerable.

Then, without warning, she flipped her spotlight off me. One thing about Mom: She doesn't keep on and on and on at any one time. Her advice comes more like a faucet drip than a thunderstorm.

"What do you think about ordering copies of this paperback for my grad students who can't write yet?" She held the catalog toward me. "Or maybe your English teacher, Mrs. Wolenhueter, has some good reference books she can recommend? Something really simple and to the point about organizing a composition?"

This was her way of ending the conversation. She doesn't like to contemplate my weakness. I took the catalog and read the description. This was my way of saying I forgave her for interfering.

"Sounds okay. At least it's cheap." I laid the catalog back on the desk. "I think I'm going on home, now. You want me to start some dinner?"

She shook her head. "I'll bring some hamburgers."

Before I was out the door, she added, "I'm sorry, honey. I really am. I didn't know they'd tell the girls I was the one who phoned. Not that I wouldn't tell them to their faces that they were acting like a couple of fools. Why don't you call Tina, and we'll go to a movie after dinner?"

I nodded and walked out the door. Geraldine continued to peck away on my mother's bibliography to a paper for the *PMLA Journal.*

chapter five

Tina called Sunday to say she'd seen Rob in Burger King with Kathi and Melinda. They hadn't arrived together, because she saw them leave in separate cars, but Tina had overheard Kathi ask Rob if he would bring her books home from school so she could stay up on homework during her suspension.

So much for why Rob hadn't called me over the weekend. Nor had Jared. But him, I didn't want to encourage. His "You won't have to bother with me anymore" had been just for attention, I was sure. *Look,* I kept telling myself, *you're not responsible for Jared.* What did he expect from me, anyway? He had a telephone.

Monday morning I walked into school, braced for the worst. One day at a time, I kept telling myself, one day at a time. But why should I be the one to be embarrassed? I hadn't gotten drunk and made the team look like a busload of lushes.

Yet no matter how I tried to rationalize, my fear hung on. How could you keep a low profile with teammates? Melinda and Kathi would certainly see about that, even from home. And besides, they had had all weekend to spread the word about my mother calling.

If someone said something to me about it, I'd made up my mind to try to laugh it off, to pretend that it was some freak hang-up with her. After all we'd been through with Grandmother's alcoholism, I couldn't blame her for her attitude about drinking; but why had she tackled this situation as if it were a personal vendetta? If Kathi and Melinda got their kicks from vodka and orange juice on a basketball bus, what was that to her? Never mind what my pastor or Matt Corley would say to my laissez-faire attitude; right now, all I could handle was uninvolvement.

Whether out of sympathy, agreement, kindness, or ignorance, few kids said anything to me about Kathi's suspension during the first few periods. But after last-period PE, when I would get benched, they would all hear the details.

As we started to change for gym, Wendy said, "Are you going to get benched?"

"I don't know. Probably."

"We might as well not suit up Tuesday night, then."

I smiled to thank her for the show of confidence, but I felt about as hollow as the gym floor.

"You and Rob go somewhere this weekend?"

"Who told you we were dating?"

She shrugged. "I don't know. Somebody."

"No, we didn't."

"You should go with him. He's cute."

As if *I* were the one who'd make that decision?

"I heard about your mother and Kathi and Melinda."

"Yeah, well, I didn't have anything to do with it."

"They're pretty mad."

Trying to hold my breath because I'd forgotten to bring clean gym clothes back after the weekend, I yanked on my sweats and walked out of the dressing room quickly, to get it over with.

Coach Charba stood at the far end of the court, looking at the score book. I had the sinking feeling I wasn't going to do what

Mother had suggested. How could I tell Coach I didn't like the restriction? Say that my mother thought the rule was silly? No matter how I worded it, I would sound like a smart aleck.

I ducked my head as I started across the court and hoped Coach hadn't seen me walk past her, but she was difficult to ignore. Not that her size commands attention; she's only five-two and has pert features, tiny wrists and ankles. But what she lacks in size, she makes up for in presence. And she can dribble like a Harlem Globetrotter.

Maybe Mother was right: Benching was too strong a punishment. Maybe I should say something to Coach. After all, there were emergencies. And for all I knew, Thursday night could have been one. Jared was too unpredictable. He'd done some stupid things in his crazy moods, like trying to ride one of their spirited horses without a saddle, and driving recklessly and fast out on farm-to-market roads full of sharp curves.

I trotted to the other end of the court, where the forwards were shooting jump shots. Out of the corner of my eye, I could see Coach start in my direction. Just as we met at center court, a ball darted between us, and I batted it back toward Brenda Andrus, a second-string player who can't dribble more than twice without losing the ball.

The coach looked at me for a long moment. "We might as well mark this game off, hadn't we?"

I shrugged and studied the scuff marks on the floor made by variously patterned tennis shoes.

"Melinda's out for the next one, too," she added.

Maybe she wasn't even going to discuss it; maybe she would just tell me I was benched, and that would be that.

"I hate to do this," she continued. "But you know—all of you know—what I've said about keeping your mind on the game. Especially *that* game."

I nodded and traced another pattern with my toe.

"I had hoped you'd be high-point this season for the district. But missing a game makes that doubtful. I haven't said anything to you about it, but you've got a good chance of being named All-State."

I glanced up to see if she was serious. She was. "I'm just a sophomore."

"It happens. Don't get your hopes up. A chance, I said."

Fat chance. A sophomore? I'd never even considered All-State.

Coach continued, "I'd like to overlook what happened—your sneaking out—I really would. But we've got to think ball if we intend to get out there and play. You've let me and your teammates down."

I had let her down? What about Kathi and Melinda?

Everything got quiet in the gym for a split second. Coach yelled for them to begin shooting free throws. With them idly standing around the free-throw line, I knew they'd be watching Coach and me, trying to hear what she was saying. I was almost glad for the benching. Maybe it would satisfy Kathi and Melinda's penchant for getting even. The ball bounced between Coach and me again; this time she leaned away and batted it back to Brenda..

"You do understand the reason behind the rule?" she probed.

"I guess." I felt sorry for her. She wanted to win as much as we did. Her left eye was blinking from a nervous twitch. It always did that during games, close ones especially. Although we call her Charba the Barber, most of us like her and play hard for her.

"Do you have anything at all to say about it? In your own defense?"

I stood there for a moment longer, staring at the scuff marks. "I guess not."

At that she raised her eyebrows.

"I mean, I'm sorry and all. That Mother called. I just wish it had been somebody else besides Melinda and Kathi who got in trouble."

"Being teammates will make it a little more difficult. But I don't think they know for sure your mother was the one who phoned us."

"Oh, they know, all right."

Coach Charba shrugged. But I knew what I was talking about; the locker scene flashed across my mind. Some people have this sixth sense about things, and Kathi was one of them. The only question was, when and how did she plan to even the score?

There was a long silence.

"I'm sorry you're going to miss the next game. But if you do well from now on, keep your mind on the game instead of your boyfriend, then you've still got a chance as high-point scorer for the season."

"Jared's not my boyfriend."

"That's all," she said. She stuck the whistle in her mouth and loped across the court.

Just as I turned to take my place at the free-throw line, I saw Rob standing in the gym doorway.

I tried to ignore him. Tina bounced the ball to me and I reached for it, fumbling it between my legs, Brenda Andrus style. I took my first shot and missed.

Rob probably thought I'd lied to him Friday morning in the office lobby, playing dumb about the Vodka Caper. If he hadn't heard about my part in the suspension while he was away at the tournament, no doubt Kathi had filled him in on any missing details.

I held the ball perched on the palm of my left hand, took one long step backward then forward as I pushed the ball off with my right hand. Again the ball bounced off the rim.

Brenda Andrus rebounded it and pushed it back to me for the next shot. Without taking my eyes from the goal, I took a second, third, and a fourth shot before finally dropping it through. All I could think about was Rob standing in the doorway, watching. And Kathi and Melinda getting even. Casually, as the next ball hit the rim and bounced away from me, I chased it and managed to glance at the doorway. He was gone.

Coach outlined our new defensive strategy, and then the team scrimmaged for the last half of the period. Coach sent me to the other end for basket practice and worked Corrie in my place. Practice lasted an eternity.

But when I came out of the gym door on my way home, Rob sat on top of an overturned garbage can, waiting for me.

chapter six

"Did I make you nervous?" he asked.

"No," I lied. "It just wasn't one of my better days."

That was just like him, thinking I couldn't keep my mind on what I was doing when he was around. Was every boy so arrogant? I thought of Jared and decided not to nix the whole gender with one sweeping generalization. Jared had enough inferiority feelings for all of them combined.

"Have you been waiting out here all this time?" I asked.

"Are you kidding? Now if the garbage can had a back to it . . . you know, stadium-seat type." He held up his hands to demonstrate.

"You want a ride?" he asked.

"Sure."

We headed for his car, parked across the now-deserted parking lot. He drives a Honda Accord that he bought with the money he earned as a summer gofer for an architectural firm. He held the door open for me, and I slid into the front seat.

"I heard on the announcements this morning that you took first place in UIL Friday."

"What did I tell you?" he shrugged, grinning. "Marked every one of those little black dots."

"Don't tell me: You left your answer sheet inside the test booklet." He smiled. "You didn't make announcements second period."

"It would have been a little awkward congratulating myself."

"Oh, I don't know, politicians do it all the time. Was Schroeder pleased? Does he get a salary bonus for his protégés that win competitions?"

"No, he just gets to keep his job another year."

We pulled into my driveway, four short blocks from the school. Rob turned off the ignition and turned to face me.

"You want to come in?" I asked. He followed me into the kitchen and stood watching me try to break the ice cubes apart.

"They always freeze together after falling in the bucket. I break a fingernail a day trying to yank them apart, but repairmen cost an arm and a leg—my mother's words." I held the clump of ice cubes out to him. "She uses a lot of clichés, for an English prof. In fact, that's why I won't let her proofread my compositions anymore."

"I'd jump at the chance. She want to read mine?" Knuckles white from the cold and pressure, he finally pulled the cubes apart and handed them back.

"You wouldn't want her to. She only *talks* clichés; I don't mean she *writes* them. That's why she doesn't read my papers anymore. She crosses out whole sentences, like you wouldn't believe. She takes out anything that sounds well-worn."

"Like *interesting* or *nice?*"

"You've got it. She's always penciling in substitutes that I've never heard of, like *poignant* and *esoteric.*"

"Still sounds like a good deal to me. I may call her up some night at midnight."

"That wouldn't bother her. She stays up all hours anyway. You'd think three classes and nine grad students would keep her busy, but they don't. Of course, she may have lots of time on her hands, once she gets fired for organizing the TAs against the university administrators."

"Sounds like she's my kind of woman."

I only smiled. I thought of Kathi's hair-code petitions last year. Mother was probably right; boys nowadays weren't interested in helpless females. But neither did I consider myself helpless—just rational. I intended to stay out of Kathi's way, and hoped she intended to stay out of mine.

"So don't you have anything else to say about the tournament?" I changed the topic. "Like how you beat out two hundred other contestants? Or was it three hundred?"

"Didn't keep count. But like I said, once they make up their minds to take me on, it's bad news. I don't have time to train them all." He grinned.

Arrogance was just the image Rob liked to project, but he really did have every right to be conceited. He was one of the rarities who had a brain but didn't act like one in class. Tina had world history with him, and she said he always sat in the back and worked on his student-council projects until Martindale called on him. Then he looked up and had to have the question repeated. And he never volunteered answers in class. This didn't get Rob any brownie points with Martindale, but it sure removed the "brain" stigma from him.

Rob makes *A*'s without even having to listen in class. He's got an analytical mind and can come up with options as good as the teachers', while most of us have to have the teachers explain the significance of what we supposedly have read.

He took his Coke and followed me into the family room, where I put on an album. We stretched out on the floor in front of the stereo.

"You sure your mom doesn't mind me being here?"

"She'll probably never ask. She's still working on that *PMLA* article."

"So you're used to having boyfriends over frequently in the middle of the day?"

I re-examined his expression. What could I have said or done to make him think I have boys over all the time? If anything, I'm conservative in my love life. In fact, my mother's a lot more liberal in her views about dating and sex than I am.

"I told you that Saturday night that I wasn't dating anyone," I repeated.

"That's what you said."

He picked up the album and began to read the back. It was an Amy Grant album, and I was pretty sure he hadn't heard of her. He finished reading and looked up.

"I think what we really need to do to spice up the yearbook this year is add a Who's Who section."

I relaxed, glad he was off the other boyfriend line of questioning. "That'd be a good idea. Though I'm surprised at you, because its not a *novel* idea. Davia Crawford wrote that they had that out in Bromley."

"Where?"

"Bromley. You remember Davia. She moved out there last summer, to live with her grandmother."

"Oh, yeah. How does she like it out there?"

"She doesn't, I don't think. She says it's hard to work her way into things. I think she's afraid to get involved in this big school board controversy they're having over creation and evolution and a textbook."

"Book. Which reminds me: Yearbook. Back to the Who's Who idea. Ours would be different, even if it's not completely original. It wouldn't have all the routine entries, like Who's Who in Chemistry or English."

"Why not? You're just afraid you wouldn't make it for any of those categories," I teased.

"What do you mean?" He pretended offense, then shrugged. "But I'd be a little embarrassed to have my picture in every category."

I grinned, and he leaned slightly closer to me. I could smell his cinnamon breath.

"No," he continued, "what I was thinking was some odd categories, for laughs. Like Who's Who in Tardies. Some legitimate ones, too, of course, like who got the most home runs this year, who drives the best-looking car. Like Kathi: Who got the drill-team hair code lifted?"

I tried to keep my face expressionless. If he wanted to put her picture in the yearbook and celebrate her getting her way when nobody in the school ever had before, let him. I moved away from him a little.

"Whose picture would you put in there—hers, or yours again?" I asked, trying to sound only mildly interested and flippant. "If I remember right, you joined her bandwagon, didn't you? You helped her get the petitions signed."

"You've got a point, but I think I'd let her have the honor on that."

Rob had joined Kathi's protest on the grounds that the students hadn't had a say when the dress requirements were instituted. He'd helped her get the petitions around the school. Of course, the drill team had lived with the code for five years with no one ever complaining—at least not publicly—and all the girls had certainly known about the code when they decided to try out.

In my opinion, if Kathi didn't want to abide by the requirements, she shouldn't have tried out. But then that's where I'm strange, I guess. I don't go in for being against everything on general principles. I thought—at least by the way Rob ran the student-council discussions—that he felt the same way.

"By the way, I heard Kathi and Melinda got suspended Friday," he said after a minute, with a nonchalant glance in my direction.

"I thought you knew they were going to. You mentioned it before I went into Mr. Timmons's office, remember?" Was he playing games—trying to see how much I really had to do with it?

"Yeah, but I didn't know for sure it was them. I talked to Kathi later at Burger King."

"I guess she told you that it was my mother who called the coach?"

"Yeah, she mentioned that," Rob said, looking me straight in the eye. If Kathi knew for sure about my part in the whole thing, it was just a matter of time.

"I didn't know she was going to call the school." I searched Rob's face for understanding. He didn't say anything.

"I guess you heard I got benched for the next game?"

"No."

"Coach has this rule that we can't talk to boyfriends,"—I tried not to look horrified at my slip—"friends or anybody." Then, to sound flippant, I added, "You know Murphy's Law: If anything can go wrong, it will."

Rob sat up straighter, put down the album he'd been dangling between his knees, and fixed his blue eyes on me. They were exactly the shade of his sky blue velour shirt. His expression was both tender and intense; I couldn't tell what he was thinking.

"You mentioned this guy Friday. Jared." His tone was flat and noncommittal.

"Yeah."

"You didn't say what was so urgent that you had to get benched for talking to him."

"As it turned out, nothing was urgent," I tried to explain. "If I'd known Coach would catch me, I certainly wouldn't have been so stupid as to ruin my chance at All-District. Missing a whole game's points will wipe me out for the season averages."

"What's his last name? Does he go to school here?"

"Sahol. He lives across Highway Sixty-Six. He's in the Brimble district. His dad works with my dad; that's how we met."

I waited. His eyes were still locked on mine, as if probing my expression to understand what I *wasn't* saying.

"Something you couldn't discuss inside the building after the game?" Rob prodded.

"He's . . . he just acts strange sometimes." I felt like a traitor, but I continued, "He's kind of a loner, and he doesn't like to come to the games, where there are a lot of kids around that he doesn't know. He only comes if it's a big game and if I insist."

"If you insist?"

"Which I don't. Not very often."

Rob lifted his eyebrows.

"You're making me feel like I have something to hide. . . ."

"Do you?"

"No." We'd had one date. Who did he think he was, to make me drop an old friendship as soon as he snapped his fingers?

But something else made me want to clutch on to Rob, to not let him walk out of my life. He was funny, articulate, good-looking, and he shared my values. At least I'd thought so; now I wasn't so sure.

"Like I said Friday, if you're going with someone else, I don't want to interfere."

"Jared and I've been best friends since seventh grade." I sounded a little exasperated. "We're . . . we're like brother and sister."

Rob said nothing, just stared.

"Most people can't understand that, I realize," I continued. "Even Tina thinks it's weird. But Jared and I have been through a lot together."

Rob's eyes held me fast, expressionless.

I continued, "And we knew each other just after my parents divorced. We've been there for each other, you know what I mean?"

After a moment, he said, "It sounds more than brother-sister, if you ask me."

I didn't respond, but got up to get us more ice. This time he didn't follow me.

When I came back into the room, he asked, "Have you ever gone to a movie together? Things like that?"

"Well, sure. . . ."

"Has he ever kissed you?"

That made me angry. I mean, first of all, the kiss didn't mean anything, except to complicate a perfectly good friendship. But Rob wouldn't understand that. I hadn't cross-examined him about his girlfriends. I hadn't even asked him why Kathi thought she had the right to request his taxi service for her books. For all I knew, he still liked her.

"Look, I'm not pushing you," Rob said. "Don't get me wrong. I'm no Rudy Curbow, expecting to have a slave following me around, devoted to my happiness for life."

I nodded that I understood. Comparing Rob to Rudy Curbow was like saying Michael J. Fox reminded you of a Mafia don. Rudy gave me the shudders, just thinking about him.

Rob continued, "I'm not the kind of guy who's going to walk up and tell you to drop everything else for me. Like I said that Saturday night, when I really like someone, I want the feeling to be mutual. I don't want to have to worry who she's talking to on the phone and if she's available on Friday nights."

"I understand that."

"I really want to get to know her—to share things with her. No secrets. I'm basically selfish when it comes to women."

"But you didn't even phone me this weekend," I protested, puzzled that his words didn't really match his actions.

He raised his Coke to his lips and finished it off before he got up to return the glass to the kitchen. When he came back, his whole expression had changed.

"Well, what do you think about the Who's Who idea?" He acted as if the rest of our conversation had never taken place.

"Sounds fine," I lied. I felt sure the whole thing had been a test, to get my reaction to Kathi. *And he accused me of playing games?*

He glanced at his watch and handed the album cover back to me. "I've got to go."

I followed him to the door. "Thanks for the ride."

He paused before letting himself out and turned back to me. "Let me know when you've worked things out with Jared."

chapter seven

If Rob wanted me to straighten out things with Jared, I would. I phoned him, again and again. There either was no answer or the housekeeper said he was out. Finally, I weaseled a little more out of her.

"This is Leanne, isn't it?"

"Yes. Can't you tell me specifically *when* I can catch him?"

"Well, his dad wasn't too happy about his grades this time."

"So is Jared there, or not?"

"They had words again."

"Has Jared left?"

"No, not that. He's just. . . ."

"What? Look, Mary, you can tell me."

"I'm worried, that's all. He just stays in his room or goes out with the horses."

"Well, I don't know why he won't call me back."

"Can't you come over and try to talk to him? I could prepare you dinner tonight."

"I've got a game."

"Well," there was disappointment in her tone, "I'll just tell him you called again."

"Thanks. I really do need to talk to him."

The score was lopsided by halftime. Peoria had us, 26–15. Everybody knew I was a starter, and if I wasn't playing when the team was behind, there had to be a good reason. I sat on the bench trying to be invisible.

Tina caught me at the water fountain during halftime and told me what she'd heard in the rest room. If it weren't for her eavesdropping, I'd be completely ignorant.

"Did you know that Kathi's parents were at school today? I bet they're going to get her permission to take all the exams she missed during suspension."

"She's coming back Friday anyway. That's five days."

"But being back doesn't mean she can take make-ups for the exams. The five days won't cost her a thing. That burns me up! Anybody else would have to take it tough and get zeros."

I shrugged.

Just then two girls I didn't know walked up and asked, "Do you mind if we get in line in front of you? We're in a hurry."

I minded, but I stepped back and let them in. So much for assertiveness.

Tina continued, "She'll get away with it, just like she did over the hair code. Her dad will threaten to sue the school board again, and they'll give her those blasted exams."

Tina pulled her shirttail out and retucked it. Anything looked good gathered around her twenty-two-inch waist. She continually walked around her house carrying little weight pads, the three-pound bags that you strap on. Whenever we talked on the phone and she sounded out of breath, I could always visualize her holding the receiver with one hand while bouncing the weights up over her head with the other.

Tina continued. "But, anyway, that's not what I started to tell you. The good news is that Kathi is running for cheerleader next year."

"That's good news? Why would it be good news to me that Kathi's running for cheerleader?"

"You are sooooo dense! You work in the office, remember?"

"So?"

"So, you'll get in on the vote counting." She winked in a knowing way, and I caught her drift.

"Look, chances of me counting votes for those elections are about one in twenty aides. Anyway, I don't have the nerve to do what you're thinking." My hesitation was over more than nerve; basically I'm an honest person.

"Oh, you'll have the nerve by the time Kathi gets through with you," Tina continued. "You just don't know what they'll try to do to you when they get back to school. You think their lying about the vodka was bad? You haven't seen anything yet!"

I didn't doubt that. Tina was overly dramatic, but I knew she was right. Over the weekend someone had actually egged my house, and I was sure Kathi was responsible. Even my mother, as shocked as she pretended to be, recognized that. Mother had put on her grubbies and gone out to scrub the sidewalk, windows, and doors herself. But I couldn't let her do it all alone. Although at first I was tempted, remembering that it was her call that had gotten me into this in the first place.

The yolks had dried in the bright early morning sun before we'd noticed the damage. Each yellow blotch had to be scrubbed with a wire brush; then it took gushes of water to squirt off the sticky residue. We both worked until almost three o'clock to get the yuck off. Part of the trim would have to be repainted, due to the scrubbing.

Kathi and Melinda had few limits or qualms—about anything. I'd seen them drive Ms. Ballantine literally to tears with their smart-aleck questions. Once they got into her creative writing class, they kept making cracks to Ms. Ballantine about her credentials, implying she wasn't qualified to teach the course because she had never published anything. Melinda and Kathi had absolutely no mercy.

I reconsidered Tina's warning. She was right. Kathi and Melinda wouldn't let me off by simply egging my house.

It was our turn at the water fountain, finally. The two girls who'd asked to get in line in front of me meandered off as if they had all the time in the world. Back on the bench, I listened to Coach give instructions, because somewhere in the back of my mind, I had the faint hope that if the score got lopsided enough, she'd send me in. I was two points under Varrington's center forward for the season. I knew missing this game would probably put me out of the running for district high-point scorer. No big deal, I tried to tell myself. I was only a sophomore; nothing really mattered until I was a senior and scholarships were at stake.

The game resumed. Everyone around us periodically stood and yelled.

"What did Rob think about the benching?" Tina asked at one of the noisiest interludes.

"He didn't say much about it. He just wanted to know who I cared enough about to sneak out of the gym to see."

Brenda Andrus stumbled over a rebound that came right to her, fumbled around, and then came up with the ball. The crowd yelled at her to hold onto the ball, as if she'd fumbled it on purpose. For the first time, I realized how stupid some of the comments from the stands sounded. It's a good thing I never heard any of them when I was on the court.

Tina whispered again, "Did he tell you he wasn't going to show up tonight?"

"No."

"If hanging around with Jared is going to scare Rob off, I'd certainly tell Jared to get lost."

"Ti . . . na," I drew out her name in exasperation, "I told you Jared and I are not going together. We're just good friends."

"Maybe in *your* mind, but not in Jared's. I saw the way he

looked at you when I was over there riding with you two that day."

There was a silence. "Look, I told you we went through this . . . relationship this summer. But it didn't work. We've got something different: no bells, no thumping hearts, no sweaty palms. We're friends. I kind of feel responsible for him, you know?"

Tina's eyes grew rounder, in her overly dramatic way. "I keep thinking about the way he looked that night at Brimble High. He was so depressed, staring off in space. Is he suicidal, do you think?"

"No!" I snapped. I didn't feel as positive as I sounded.

"Then why don't you forget him?"

"I just feel responsible for him, that's all."

"You mean you're not going to drop Jared *unless* Rob says," Tina chirped.

"Unless nothing," I contradicted her. "What I feel for Rob has nothing to do with what I feel about Jared. Rob ought to know that."

"You're stubborn, do you know that?"

I shrugged. Tina sure didn't know me as well as I thought. I guess Mother's right; I don't spill my guts often enough. But that's what was so special about Jared and me. With him, I did. My eyes filled up, and I didn't know why. This had been the longest ten days of my life.

I looked back to the court. Corrie made a really long shot, and the bench stood up and yelled in unison. We were within ten points of Peoria now.

I thought of Saturday night a week ago and how I had returned Rob's kiss. That night Rob seemed to be everything I'd been looking for in a guy.

Of course, we'd had a little head start in that we knew each other from student council. We were always the first two to show up for the before-school meetings. He has this thing, he says, about not asking any of the members to do anything he wouldn't do himself, including getting to school on Monday morning at 7:00 A.M. So why was he expecting me to drop Jared as a friend when he was hanging around Kathi?

At first meeting, Rob comes off like a politician, pumping hands and promising rainbows. But you soon learn he is much more. He really intended to keep the promises he made—or work his head off trying. Actually, he'd accomplished quite a lot, given the limited clout the administration allowed the council. He had led several major fund-raising drives to buy things only the student body cared about having—more trophy cases and a bigger sign in front of the building for displaying witty or appropriate slogans about school activities. And he'd led a charity drive for toys at Christmas for the underprivileged. He'd done a lot for school spirit—not an easy task when the students came from four different junior highs around town.

In the mornings, while waiting for everybody else to drag in, we always talked about schoolwork and council projects, then got into more personal things. Sometimes I told him about the weekends my father was in town and our visits. One morning we even got into divorce and how we'd never marry until we were sure. Rob has given it as much thought as I have because his brother-in-law ducked out on his older sister right after she'd finished putting him through medical school. He commented one morning that he wouldn't ask a girl to give up her future for him; he planned to wait until he could support a family before he married.

Talking about serious things that mattered was one of the really nice things about Rob—and Jared. You can't do that with most guys; they tease and never take anything seriously. I decided that Jared and Rob were a lot alike, in some ways, except that Jared took his seriousness as a fault, like he did with everything else he hated about himself. Rob saw his own tendency to be serious as desirable maturity.

Corrie took the ball out of bounds and made a bad pass that was intercepted and turned into a basket. Tina said, "You are kidding, aren't you, about continuing to see Jared if Rob asks you not to?"

"Rob hasn't asked me not to." I was telling the truth; he hadn't outright asked.

"But you know how he feels," Tina pressed.

"All I know is that I don't intend to drop my old friends just because Rob says so. For all I know, he may not even intend to ask me out again."

I didn't feel quite as determined as I sounded to Tina. I wanted Rob, all right, but at the cost of losing Jared's friendship?

If the egging hadn't evened the score in Kathi's mind and she decided to get into the middle of things with Rob, maybe I wouldn't even have to make that decision.

"Frankly, I don't see that the student council has anything to say about how we do the yearbook." Tim Lacey never was one for tact. It didn't faze him that he made his comment in front of all the council members. He stretched his arms behind his head and leaned his chair back against the wall. The chair slid on the freshly waxed floor, and Tim caught himself just before his head cracked against the wall. Everybody laughed.

"Well, I just thought it was an idea," Rob said. "That's probably the only way Fitz Germany will ever make a name. How many days has he cut this year? Maybe it'd be easier to count the days he's been here. I mean, guys like him should get recognized for *something*."

Tim, red-faced, untangled himself from his chair and stood up.

"Yeah," somebody else spoke up, "I think it's a good idea. I could think of a few Who's Whos I'd like to get in there."

"I didn't say it wasn't an interesting idea," Tim snapped. "I just said the student council didn't have anything to do with it."

I knew what Tim was driving at. The yearbook was his claim to fame, and he resented Rob's intrusion on his turf.

Tim added, "Rob seems to have enough on his hands, running

the rest of this place. He can let us little guys make a few decisions." The others around the table now got the picture, and things got tense.

"I wasn't trying to tell you—or anybody else on the yearbook staff—what to do. It was an idea. Take it or leave it," Rob said.

"We'll leave it," Tim said as he jerked the chair upright and stalked off.

"What's with him?" somebody asked.

Nobody answered. "Well, I think the Who's Who thing would be funny," someone finally said.

"That's not the point. Tim wanted the student council out of it altogether."

"The student council's not in it," Rob said. "Can't a guy make a suggestion? Forget it. Just forget it."

Mrs. Wolenhueter pretended to be invisible. She was good at that, the kind of sponsor I liked, even though she was disorganized and called the entire second-period roll every day. Her presence was enough to keep things reasonably under control, but she still let us run the show.

"Here, Leanne." Nick shoved a pen and paper toward me. "You take notes."

"I did it last time."

"So? You're a girl. Girls have better handwriting."

"That's a sexist statement," Karen Kollar said.

"You want to take them, then?" He shoved the paper toward her.

"You're a jerk. Did you know that?"

When Karen shoved the pen and paper back, I gave in and started writing the attendance record and the date. *Why did I always let people push me into things?* I didn't know then and I still don't.

Before we came up with anything more constructive than the Who's Who idea, the meeting broke up, and everybody bolted off to their lockers before the bell sounded and halls jammed with incoming students. That was one advantage of having to get to school for early morning meetings; at least you got to your locker without getting trampled.

I took my time getting out. I could feel Rob's gaze as I gathered up my notebook and put the minutes away.

"Did you win last night?" Rob was at my side as we left the room and headed for the lockers.

"Afraid not. Forty-eight to twenty-eight."

"Hmmmm."

"My sentiments, exactly." I wanted to keep things light. "I didn't see you there."

"No."

I waited. I supposed that was intended to be a message to me. Rob always attended all the games.

"About Tim," he continued. "Did you get the picture I was trying to tell him how to run his yearbook?"

"No. That's just Tim. We should look into the idea of sending him to a home for the incurably obnoxious."

He laughed. "I just don't want to get out of line and have him think I'm crowding him. He's dependable, and he has some good ideas."

I smiled reassuringly. This was the real Rob, sensitive enough to care about hurting people's feelings.

"Kick me under the table or splatter me with a leaky Bic if you see me stepping out of bounds again."

"Sure. It's just Tim, really."

As we approached the door, I turned to the left, and he turned to the right. "See you," he said, as if he were talking to just anyone rather than to someone he had kissed only twelve days ago.

"Yeah, see ya." I glanced in his direction just long enough to see Kathi waiting for him at the corner.

chapter eight

I gave up on Jared returning my calls. One more try, and I was done with it all.

"Oh," he answered unenthusiastically, "Leanne."

"Hello," his dad's husky voice came over the line on the extension.

"I got it, Dad," Jared said.

"Finally!" his dad said. But there was no click from the extension being hung up.

I had the uneasy feeling I was about to be caught in the crossfire. Should I say something to remind them of my presence on the other end of the line?

"Well, is it for you or me?" His dad harumphed.

"For me."

"Well, I'm tempted to stay on the line. A girl? Maybe we should record this." His dad snorted a half-laugh and then clicked off the line before finding out if his assumption was correct.

Silence.

"Jared, you still there?"

"I'm here."

Silence again. I felt mortified. *What was with his dad?* As far as I could tell, and from all Matt Corley had helped me sort out, Mr. Sahol had reached emotional detachment from his wife even before her actual death. It had really been just Jared and his mother, at the last. I preferred to think his dad couldn't face seeing her get weaker every day, rather than think he was an insensitive clod. Jared and I had spent the most time with Mrs. Sahol at the very end, bringing her ice cubes to keep in her mouth, bathing her face to keep her comfortable.

But why was Mr. Sahol doing this to Jared?

I tried to relieve Jared's embarrassment by avoiding the whole topic. "I've been trying to call you."

"I know."

"This semester going all right?"

"Yeah, it's okay. Teachers are okay."

"Good."

Silence.

"I thought you'd like Brimble, once you got into things."

He gave a long sigh. "Yeah. I'm considering running for class president."

I ignored the sarcasm. "Your dad's in town for a while, I guess?"

"Yeah."

Silence.

"We lost to Peoria."

"Really?"

"I didn't get to play."

"Yeah. I remember."

"No big deal, I guess. No scholarship at stake this year. Probably lets me out for district high point, though."

"Yeah. I'm sorry."

"No, it's okay. Really."

Silence.

"Well, look, I guess I'll let you go. I just called to see if everything was okay."

"Yeah. You and Rob still dating?"

"Not since that Saturday night. One date."

"Hmmm."

I had mixed emotions about discussing that whole subject with Jared. Adding that I wished Rob *had* called would let Jared know I really meant what I said about our just being friends. But it also might be the comment that would underscore what his dad had just not so subtly done to him. So I decided to leave it at that.

"Well, listen, call me sometime. My backhand's getting lousy," I said.

"Yeah, sure."

"Have you been playing much?"

"No."

The other extension clicked, and his dad's voice came back on. "Jared, are you still on the phone?"

"Yes."

"Well, unless you're talking to the Princess of Monaco, get off. I need to call Caroline." Click.

Before I hung up, Jared said, "Leanne, thanks. For calling, I mean."

Jared didn't sound okay, and his dad's implication that he was a total outcast incapable of making friends really hit me. *Who did his dad think he was?* After all, how many popularity contests had he won? Just because he tried to dress like a teenager didn't mean he looked like one. Frankly, I had never thought Mr. Sahol was half as good-looking as he seemed to think he was. No wonder Jared had zero confidence in himself.

I couldn't decide if I felt better or worse after the phone call. To give you an idea about my state of mind during these two weeks, my dentist appointment proved to be a high point.

I had taken the car to school that day so I could chauffeur myself around. My appointment was at 8:00, as early as possible, so I wouldn't have to miss any more of first period than absolutely necessary. Mr. Blackley was supposed to be reviewing for a biology test, and he practically gives away all the answers. I got up extra early and was waiting outside the dentist's office when the nurse got there at 7:45 to open up. The dentist wasn't in yet, but he would be with me in a few minutes. About 8:10 a man in a business suit came in and harumphed around until the nurse slid back her windowed cage and asked if she could help him.

"Charles Wittman," he introduced himself. "I have an appointment at eight-fifteen, and I hope it's not a minute later, because I have a client coming in at ten."

"Oh. I'll see what I can do. The doctor just came in. Maybe we can get you right in."

He stood waiting, looked around at me, and gave me a tight smile.

The receptionist came back to the desk and leaned up to the window. "Leanne, would you mind if we worked Mr. Wittman in ahead of you? I'm sure you're not exactly in a hurry to get back to school, are you?"

"Well, sort of. I. . . ."

"Thank you."

Mr. Wittman didn't bother to glance at me before darting through the door to the inner sanctum. After he was halfway down the hall, the receptionist leaned closer to the window. "Do you mind?"

I glared at her in my most threatening manner. If the man had waited all night, what would another fifteen minutes matter? I cleared my throat and tried to sound authoritative. "I do need to get back as soon as possible. I have a test."

"Oh, well, we'll hurry then." She closed her cage window.

So much for my attempt at assertiveness. No wonder I couldn't get anything out of Jared; I wasn't exactly a threat to the legal profession.

When Mother came in from work, I had fajitas ready, but the dinner conversation didn't help my mood any.

"You have anything planned for tonight?" she asked when we sat down to the table.

"No."

"Rob hasn't called lately, has he?"

"No."

"You aren't still putting him off because of Jared's problems, are you? Still feeling responsible for him?"

I put down my fork and looked her in the eye. "Doesn't plain old friendship count for something anymore?"

She didn't answer me, and we finished in silence.

I moped around the house the rest of the evening and went to bed feeling as though Tina and Mother were conspiring to confuse me about the issues.

Just before bedtime, I phoned Matt Corley, and his wife got on the extension, too. It was a little hard to hear over their crying baby, but they said enough to reassure me I hadn't lost my perspective. God hadn't put me in Jared's life just to desert him when things got a little crazy. While I had Matt on the line, I confessed a big, festering attitude about revenge where Kathi was concerned. When I hung up, I felt a little better. You do the right thing, and things turn out right. Right?

chapter nine

I pulled up the shady lane in front of Jared's house and honked the horn; he came around from the backyard. The beaten, sullen snarl I'd seen the night of the gym incident had been replaced by the old lopsided grin that I remembered from seventh grade. We stood looking at each other a little awkwardly at first, and then after a moment, he said, "You want to ride? I was just leaving."

"Sure."

I followed him through the backyard gate and out the other gate on the back side of the fence. I stood letting Cricket nibble a handful of oats while Jared saddled her. We talked about how the horses liked to get a good workout and how Jared was the only one who ever rode them anymore. The two they bought for his parents to ride hardly knew their real owner; his dad "didn't have the time." Jared was their groomer, their caretaker, their friend.

"I know what you mean," I said. "My mother has her head in books all the time. Now that the teaching assistant salary negotiations are getting nowhere, she's even busier, trying to organize them to pull off a walkout—if it comes to that. She eats, sleeps and talks it."

It was not that I minded Mother's other interests. On the contrary, I welcomed them. I certainly have enough sense to know a good role model when I see one. I only made the comment so Jared wouldn't think his father was the only parent in the world who had other things on his mind.

We rode around the shady path at a leisurely pace, talking very little. Jared's dad owned about seven acres, which had not yet been swallowed up by housing developers, at the edge of the subdivision. The seven acres were like a secluded fortress, surrounded by tall fences and thick trees and bushes. The taller trees overhung the horse trails and provided shade for most of the day. Riding around the slight declines and hills and through the narrow stream running across the property was almost like riding through a television wilderness, sans cowboys, Indians, and wild beasts.

"Cricket doing okay?" Jared called back to me. "That's a new saddle."

"It's not rubbing her. She's fine."

Jared rode about ten yards ahead of me, staying on the shady trail around the perimeter of their property. His body jostled up and down in front of me, shoulders erect and head high, quite unlike the way he'd left me that night at the game. He wore a brown plaid shirt with the long sleeves rolled up above his elbows, but no jacket, even though it was a cool February day. His tan had not faded much from the deep bronze of the fall. He was smaller than Rob, but just as nice-looking, in his own way.

I remembered the day he first kissed me. It was at the end of August, just two weeks after his mother's funeral. I hadn't been over much during that time because relatives swarmed everywhere, and I didn't want to interfere. The one or two mornings I did go over, we didn't do much beside sit around. I figured he'd know I cared just because I was there.

Earlier that summer we'd talked about death in general terms, like you do when it's not happening to people you know. He'd ask me a lot of questions about God and heaven and my beliefs. I think the fact that I was sure about what I believed gave him courage and comfort. Later, he'd asked if I thought my pastor would visit with his mother. I set things up, and both Jared and his mother became Christians before her death. Still, he was reluctant to open up with me about his feelings toward his dad, and he couldn't seem to reconcile them with his new faith.

And when his mother got really bad in the last two weeks, I couldn't think of much to say, other than the Scripture passages Matt Corley had written down for me, so I just let him talk. His father and his grandparents had one another; Jared only had me, and God.

But on that August day one week before school was to start, we had decided to play tennis for the first time since the funeral. Mary, their housekeeper, had served us Pepsi and toffee bars when we'd flopped down on the patio to rest. Jared had seemed a little more relaxed and seemed to forget for a while what he'd been through.

"Thanks," he said. I looked at him quizzically. "For the tennis," he added.

"Your courts," I shrugged.

"But your idea." I accepted his thanks. He continued, "It's hard knowing how you're supposed to act. You know what I mean?"

I didn't, really.

"Should you turn on TV? Go to a movie? Ride the horses? I don't want to be disrespectful, but I don't think Mom would mind, do you?"

I shook my head. "Your mother wouldn't have wanted you to sit around and be miserable. You've got to do something to get your mind off it. You know she wasn't like that. She would be sitting out here watching us today, if she could."

Jared nodded. Then, "Grandmother looked at me kind of funny when I said we were going outside and took my tennis racket with me."

"Everybody grieves in his own way," I said after a moment.

Jared stretched out beside the tree trunk and leaned back on the grass with his hands behind his head.

"Do your grandparents stay over here a lot now?"

"Not really. But they've been over more in the last two weeks than in the last three years we've lived here. They and my dad don't get along too well. I guess they come over for me. Maybe that's why they acted offended when we left the house just now and came out here. It's just that everybody sits around staring at me like I'm going to crack up any minute."

"Yeah. It was like that after my parents' divorce. But you can't sit around and think about things all the time. Trying to forget now and then helps." I watched him as he lay stretched out in front of me.

I took another toffee bar and leaned back against the patio curb. That wasn't too comfortable, so I edged my way off the concrete, onto the grass beside him. We lay side by side looking up into the late afternoon sun for a long time. The low branches from the oak tree offered some shade for our faces. After a while we heard his grandparents and his father talking in the front driveway. They were leaving and told his father to call if he needed anything.

"Phoning them is the last thing he'll do," Jared said, almost angrily. "He doesn't even think about her anymore."

"You don't know that, Jared. You can't know that."

He didn't say anything for a moment. "I can almost see her over there in that lounge chair."

I leaned up on my elbow and turned in the direction Jared was staring. I could see tears in his eyes.

"And she'd be laughing," I added. "She always was the best audience you ever had for your lousy backhand."

Jared had leaned up on his elbow and faced me. The tears had disappeared. He leaned toward me and kissed me on the lips, softly at first, then again harder.

"I don't know what I'd do without you," he said.

I didn't answer. I had to let what happened soak in for a moment. One kiss, and our relationship of three years had changed forever.

Just then, Jared's father had come to the patio door, seen us, and turned around to go back inside. I realized how things must have looked to him, our being stretched out side by side on the grass. Quickly, I had gotten up and mumbled something to Jared about having to leave.

Only back home in the privacy of my own room had I been able to sort through my feelings about that afternoon. The first few times we were together after that had been awkward. I began to hesitate about dropping by without a special invitation for tennis or basketball or a swim. We didn't look each other in the eye. Teasing on the tennis court didn't come as easily.

It was well into the fall before we gradually slipped into our old casual, just-friends relationship. Good-bye kisses became just a part of our routine. And it seemed as though Jared always picked the weirdest times to kiss me—usually when his father was puttering around somewhere in the background.

No fireworks, at least for me. I felt as if we were playing dress up in Mother's old clothes, kissing each other like celebrities on TV talk shows.

Once school had started, we saw each other less frequently because we went to different schools and had other things on our minds. At least, I did. I was never sure what Jared felt, until the night at the game.

Obviously, he still read more into things than I did, but I had gone through some ambivalent feelings myself. I mean, even though my palms didn't start to sweat and my heart didn't pound when he was around, I didn't rule out the possibility that maybe this was the real kind of love, rather than the romantic feelings you read about in novels. During this period, we divided our time between romantic interludes like movies and steak dinners and friendly things like grooming the horses and checking mint marks on coins he'd collected. I felt more comfortable with the latter.

But the whole thing was so confusing. We couldn't break up the romantic part without damaging the friendship part. We weren't like some couples who marked their first date as their anniversary and celebrated each month. We didn't begin; we just were.

"I'm sorry about the other night at the gym," Jared said as I pulled my horse up beside his.

"That's okay."

I was doing it again—acting like it was no big deal, like it didn't matter that I got benched and had probably lost my chance at district high-point because he couldn't wait to talk to me until after the game.

"I should have called to see what happened."

"Yeah, you should have," I surprised myself by saying.

"But I figured you wouldn't want to talk to me after I got you in trouble."

"I gave it some thought," I said, but I smiled.

"Look, I'm sorry for making you come outside."

"Forget it, it's all right."

"I just got moody, you know? On long weekends when my dad is out of town . . . well . . . I decided I had to talk to somebody who acted normal."

"What do you mean normal?"

"Not like some of the creeps that I go to school with at Brimble. They act like I came from another planet."

"Well," I gestured toward the stables that we were approaching, "you do have a slightly larger layout here than most of them."

"What does that have to do with anything?"

"How can you be best friends with someone who has triple your own allowance to spend? Maybe they're jealous. Or intimidated."

"Look, I don't go around flashing my money. You ought to know that. If anything, I hide it, despite the fact that my dad says outspending the competition is the only way I could ever get a girl."

"Well, he's wrong."

His eyes lit up. Then I clarified quickly. "I bet there are a lot of girls at your school who'd like to go out with you, if you gave them a chance."

"Name one."

"How can I? I don't know anybody over there."

"Just as well."

I stared straight ahead. Our horses tried to sideswipe each other and stopped to rub noses before moving toward the stables.

"Look," he added after a moment, "it's plain enough that you don't care anymore."

"Jared. . . ."

"No, let me finish. This isn't going to be a sob story. I'm not thickheaded: I don't have to have a crystal ball to see that our being together doesn't leave you breathless."

I started to interrupt him again, to tell him that he wasn't being fair. He held up his hand to stop me again.

"I think you could say our relationship has turned a corner."

"What do you mean?" I was both curious and surprised at his admission.

"We're back to being sensible again. If my dad is disappointed, he'll just have to give me a bigger allowance."

"What are you talking about?"

"I just told you he said I'd have to outspend the competition."

"I know what you meant by that. But what does that have to do with *me*?"

"He's part of the reason I've been trying to make our relationship something it isn't. He thinks you're good-looking and I should be man enough to hold onto you."

"You mean you've been acting like we were going together just to please your father."

"Now don't get mad. It's not like it sounds. This feels weird, you know? Telling a girl you like her because your father wants you to."

I waited for his explanation.

"You remember that my dad wanted me to stay in the private school, and we begged him to let me go to Brimble?"

I nodded.

"Well, now he throws it up to me, saying I don't fit in. He thinks I'm backward when it comes to girls. He saw me kiss you that day in the backyard this summer, and he jumped to some conclusions. I didn't see any harm in letting him think things were more serious than they were."

"So you kissed me to please your father? Now that's a twist." Was I embarrassed, or hurt? I didn't know.

"I kissed you because I wanted to. My feelings were all messed up during that time, you know?"

"How about what you said outside the gym?"

"I guess I couldn't face explaining to my father why you weren't coming around here as much. He started to ask questions about what was going on with us and if we'd broken up or something. Why wasn't I going to your games? I couldn't tell him you'd started to date Rob. He would have called me the 'twirp of the tiddledywinks set.' "

I didn't say anything.

"Look, I knew this wasn't going to come out right. That's why I haven't called in the last two weeks. I was dreading talking to you."

I glared at him. "What's that supposed to mean?"

"Straightening things out. You know. I don't want to mess up something as good as we had by confusing what we felt for each other. When I kissed you that first time last summer—and even later—I thought I loved you. I couldn't have made it through the funeral and everything afterward without you. I guess I was so confused then that I mistook friendship on your part for something more. I . . . I messed things up."

We rode along in silence for a few hundred feet. The horses plodded along together now, as if their moves had been synchronized.

"What we've got is something better, don't you think?" he asked.

I smiled and nodded.

"Are you still mad?" he asked.

"No. But you're forgiven only on one condition."

He looked concerned.

"Tell your dad that to keep my attention, you've got to have a bigger allowance—and cut me in."

"Not a bad idea."

We both laughed. I kicked my horse in the flanks, and he shot forward. Jared caught up with me, and then we slowed again.

"You know what we need to do?" I said, relieved that the whole deception was out in the open. "Have a party and get some of the kids from the two schools together. I mean, it's not like we live in foreign countries. The highway up there is the dividing line between the two school districts. Brimble and Herrington kids go to the same theaters, the same supermarkets, work after school at the same greasy spoons. Several go to our church. Why shouldn't they be friends, no matter which school they go to?"

"Are you kidding?" Jared said. "With all the rivalry between Herrington and Brimble?"

"That's just the point. That stupid rivalry is why we have so much vandalism. Of course, I think what was done the other day—did you hear about the new decor on our temporary classrooms?—was done by some of our own kids. Probably somebody that flunked this last quarter, like Rudy Curbow."

I got quiet a moment, wondering if I really believed in what I'd just said. Hosting a party for students from both schools was a little scary. What if nobody got along?

I always get carried away when I'm trying to be enthusiastic for someone else's sake. But I was sure that if I could get Jared to take a first step toward meeting some other kids, he'd find friends. He was just too shy. And the stupid comments his dad made about everybody only being interested in his money didn't help his self-confidence any.

"What kind of party?" Jared asked after a moment.

"Any kind. You know, just have a bunch of kids over to listen to records, play pool, eat—that kind of party."

"I've never been to a party. Except when I was a little kid—birthday parties and stuff like that." He looked straight ahead as he talked, pretending to concentrate on reining his horse around a tree trunk.

I was shocked. As rich as he was? His folks could have laid out a spread for a hundred without batting an eye. And with the mansion he lived in—a patio decorated like something in *House Beautiful*, a swimming pool, tennis courts, stables—he'd never given a party? Granted, his family had lived in France for most of Jared's life, but still, never to have been to a party of any kind anywhere?

I tried not to look at him, so he wouldn't feel embarrassed.

"Let's do it. What do you say?" I pressed the idea.

"Over here?"

My first impulse was to jump at the chance, but that might defeat the purpose of getting Jared some friends. Seeing such a layout, the kids might categorize him as a snob and never include him in their own parties later.

"No. Why don't we have it at my house? It's smaller, but it'd be easier to have it there if I do most of the food. Unless you want to do that?"

He looked relieved. "No. Your place it is." He was quiet a minute. "I don't know. Don't you think I should go to some parties first, just to see how it is?"

"No. You might as well start at the top, with me as your hostess."

He grinned. I circled around and began to gallop my horse toward the stables before Jared could change his mind about the party. He followed me in and began to unsaddle the horses. When he finished with the horses, we walked back toward my car in the driveway.

"I'm having second thoughts about the party, Leanne. I just can't talk to people."

"You talk to me."

"That's different."

"Why?"

"Just is."

He dropped it, but I wasn't about to let him change his mind on the party. No way would I let him down.

Just as we got to the driveway, his dad pulled up in front of the house and jaunted around to the passenger side of his Mercedes to open the door. He and a woman in her twenties strolled across the driveway and stopped as they approached us.

"Bebs, this is Jared and his girlfriend, Leanne."

Jared sheepishly stuck out his hand, and I mumbled something appropriate while trying not to stare at the way both of them were dressed. With his hair curling down past both ears, tight jeans, expensive cowboy boots, and gold chains, Jared's dad looked forty going on seventeen. Meanwhile, Bebs seemed to be playing dress-up with her mother's makeup and cocktail dress. If she'd just twirled off a dance floor somewhere, how did she pick up him, dressed like a broncobuster?

"You two give the horses a good workout?" Mr. Sahol asked.

"Yeah. An hour or so," Jared said.

"Good." He turned to Bebs. "Jared socializes with the horses about as much as he does people."

She smiled, flashing her Farrah Fawcett teeth in Jared's direction. "That's nice."

"Leanne's quite a superstar around Herrington High. Plays basketball," he said to Bebs while looking at me.

"How nice," Bebs repeated.

"If she and Jared ever get their act together, she may let Jared caddy for her someday."

"That's golf," I said, smiling faintly.

"Jared wouldn't know the difference, I don't think. Would you, son?" He flashed a plastic, much-too-large smile at Jared.

Jared, his jaw clenched, said nothing.

"Well," Mr. Sahol's smile faded and he cleared his throat, "you and Leanne aren't leaving, are you? Bebs is going to have dinner with us. I called Mary earlier to let her know we were coming. Didn't she tell you?"

"We've been out riding. I haven't been back to the house."

"I was just leaving," I spoke up to clarify where I fit into their plans.

"You can't stay? What's the matter?" Mr. Sahol cut his eyes toward Jared with a condemning glare.

"I promised my mother I'd be back to eat dinner with her."

"I see."

But clearly he didn't. He'd chalked up my unenthusiasm about staying for dinner as further evidence of Jared's failure.

He turned, looped his arm around Bebs's waist, and maneuvered her on across the lawn toward the front door.

"Listen," I said to Jared through the lowered car window, "let's have the party a week from Friday night. You have anything then?"

He smirked. "Me? That's the idea behind the party, isn't it? To get the hermit out of the woods?"

I smiled. "Not *just* for you. Remember who just gave *me* the let's-be-friends routine."

"Ah, come on." He looked at me with sheepishly downcast eyes.

I continued. "I don't exactly find parties a bore, you know. I'm always in the market for good-looking guys."

I tried to sound light, but I suppose I was testing our new relationship. Although we hadn't gone into detail about Rob during our ride, that didn't mean I'd failed to see how he would fit into the party scheme. I had an idea beginning to brew in the back of my mind, and if it worked, Rob and I might make it yet.

chapter ten

Tina liked the idea. "Who else is coming, besides Rob?"

"I didn't say Rob *was* coming," I held the phone a moment, to add to her suspense. "I said I was going to *ask* him. I just hope he doesn't have a diving meet next weekend."

"He's part of the student council, isn't he?" Tina tried to reassure me about his presence.

"Yeah. But when I phoned everybody, they didn't act too overjoyed about my purpose for the party—to improve school relations."

"Sounds about as interesting as a United Nations summit."

"Does it sound that corny?"

"I've heard better," Tina said. "And what about Jared and the two names he gave you, not to mention me and the others you said you were inviting? We're not on the council."

"So it'll be a mixture. I didn't plan that we'd sit around and compare class budgets or trophy cases. It's supposed to be fun, too."

"I sure hope this works with Rob."

"Why shouldn't it? When Rob sees that Jared is here, he'll know I wouldn't invite both of them if I were really interested in him. Right? I'll make it very clear that Jared and I are like brother and sister. And Rob will see with his own two eyes that I prefer to flirt with him and that Jared isn't jealous. Therefore Jared *couldn't* be competition. Right?"

"But what if everybody else doesn't play their lines right? What if Jared *does* get jealous and pouts and makes things worse?"

"He won't."

"I hope you're right. But getting them both under the same roof could prove to be dangerous."

"Thanks for the moral support."

We threw around a few other ideas about how to rearrange the furniture to accommodate more people and what to serve for snacks. When I hung up the phone, I felt rather pleased with myself. The party should solve both Jared's and my problems.

The night of the party, I tried not to look flabbergasted when I answered the door and saw Jared had a girl with him—a little surprise he hadn't mentioned. Perfect; that would make an even bigger impression on Rob.

Carmen Baedahl, a senior at Brimble, was tall and willowy, with a wanton expression that fit her body. She looked twenty-five. Right from the beginning, I decided she wasn't Jared's type. Was that a pang of jealousy? As soon as the introductions were over, Carmen excused herself to go comb her hair. Her pencil-thin, khaki-colored skirt stretched tightly over her hips as she swayed out of the room.

I turned to Jared. "There wasn't any need to come early, since you have a date. Your dad sent Mary over to help with the food. I didn't know you asked anybody."

"I didn't, exactly."

I waited for an explanation.

"Would you believe this is my dad's idea? We went out to the club to eat last night, and Carmen is their new hostess. He struck up a conversation with her while we waited for a table. Before I knew it, he'd suggested that I bring her to the party."

"Didn't you have a choice? I mean, she's pretty and all that, but she doesn't seem your type." It was Carmen's sophistication that I was referring to, but I didn't want to get specific. Jared already had a complex about how young he looked.

"I guess I could have stomped my foot, thrown a tantrum, and told her I had ringworm," Jared deadpanned. "But she might have thought me a little rude."

I smiled.

He added, "If it disappoints him to have a shy son, why not go along? You said I had to take risks, right?"

"She looks like a risk, all right." Mary asked me something about the ice for the Cokes, and I dropped the subject with Jared.

By eight o'clock most of the guests had arrived. The party was going well. Although Rob hadn't shown up yet, I had every confidence he would. I put Jared in charge of the albums and Cokes, to keep him from standing around looking nervous. Carmen had no trouble mingling. Evidently, she thought Tim Lacey was attractive, because she kept gravitating to his side.

I kept an eye on Jared to see how he was reacting to that, but I couldn't tell. Mostly, he read the backs of the album jackets before he put them on to play. I flitted around from one group to the other, talking about nothing and studying the door, waiting for Rob to show up.

Really, I was halfway miffed at myself for caring so much. Rob, I was certain, hadn't given me a thought in the last month. He acted like nothing had passed between us, like we were just council members discussing the next fund drive.

And what was I doing to counter that image? Throwing a party for student council members from both schools—a legitimate party with legitimate purposes. He probably thought it was a stupid idea. Well, at least the Brimble council president had been enthusiastic about swapping ideas with us. Certainly, nothing formal would take place—we wouldn't sign a peace treaty establishing spray-paint control or anything—but at least the mood would be set for a little cooperation in the future.

Mary came into the room carrying a tray of pizza slices hot from the oven. Before she got halfway across the floor, the tray was emptied. Having her come had been a good idea. One night when I'd phoned Jared about our plans, his dad had answered the phone. He talked to me a while and acted disappointed that we'd decided to have the party at our house instead of theirs. Sending his housekeeper, he insisted, was the least he could do. I couldn't very well explain to him that their house was too nice for Jared's own good, so I just let him wonder about my lack of taste and judgment.

Someone in the corner got a little loud. I glanced over to see Tim Lacey and Brimble council member Stewart Morris squaring off, as my dad always referred to it. Other conversations gradually faded out around the room, and various huddles diverted their attention to the two boys standing behind the sofa. Tim had his back to me, both hands hanging loosely at his sides. Although I couldn't see his expression, his tone told me that things could get out of hand fast.

"I didn't say it wasn't a big award," Stewart Morris said. "I just said it's not exclusive. Your pictures meet certain standards and they pin a blue ribbon on it, so to speak. No competition involved."

I gathered that they were talking about photography, and as I'd already observed from my limited acquaintance with Tim Lacey, he ate and slept photography, and the yearbook. I remembered his outburst at Rob about the Who's Who idea.

"I'd like to see some of your work," Tim said, but his tone indicated just the opposite. "You have anything with you?"

"I don't carry my portfolio around in my back pocket."

"Lots of people talk a good picture, but when it gets down to composition, that's another matter," Tim challenged.

"I've seen your yearbook. Did you do the candids?"

"Some of them, why?"

"Shadows were pretty bad on most of them."

Tim took a step closer. They stood about two feet apart, definitely within each other's space. I could feel the tension around the room; most of the students nearby had focused on the two of them. I knew I should do something quickly, but what? Basketball player or not, I wasn't the type to throw my body between two angry males, even if one of them was only slightly heavier than a straw.

"I don't exactly carry a tripod and lighting around with me, either," Tim added. He took a step closer. "Candids are candids."

Just then Mother came through the room and spoke to a few guests. The tension dissolved immediately. Tim turned and walked over to Carmen.

Mother had done it again, simply by walking into the room. Others probably thought the tension broke just because an adult entered the room, but that wouldn't do it with Tim Lacey. Adults never intimidated him. It was Mother, specifically.

At 10:05 the doorbell rang and Tina, standing by the door, answered it. Rob walked in.

I couldn't remember what I was saying to Ted Oshman. However, I must have been at the end of my sentence, because he picked up the thought and continued the dialogue. I kept stealing glances toward the door. Rob was still in the entryway, and Tina was introducing him to some of the Brimble kids.

I had to get to him before he saw Jared. At least Carmen's presence would help make my point—*if* I could catch her near enough to Jared for Rob to see she was his date. And *if* I could get Carmen to keep her paws off Tim Lacey. How obvious would it look if I handcuffed Carmen to Jared's side for five minutes and then marched Rob over to introduce them as a loving couple?

Ted Oshman finished what he was saying about how their girls' basketball team could sure use some help this season and didn't I think the girls who played were some of the best-looking in school? I smiled modestly.

"No, I'm not kidding," he insisted. "The pumping-iron commercials for women—they're great." He let out a low whistle and did a hot-momma shake.

"Well, I'm not into weight lifting." With that, I guided his attention to Tim Lacey, who was preening and pouting nearby, and made my escape.

"Glad you made it," I said as I got to Rob.

"Yeah, me, too. I wasn't sure I could. I had some other places to go tonight, too."

"Oh? What else is going on that I don't know about?"

"Nothing big, not schoolwide or anything. Just a few scattered poster parties for the cheerleader candidates."

"Oh, yeah." Smiling at my own cynicism, I tried to visualize Kathi's small, intimate poster party, to which she'd only invited her closest five hundred friends.

I didn't know any of the other candidates really well, but Lucinda Harwin had mentioned her party to me and said to come by if I had time. When any kind of election comes up, suddenly everybody is ultrafriendly.

"Come on, I'll take you around and introduce you to everybody from Brimble," I said to Rob.

"Okay." He took my hand, and we pushed our way through the group standing in the entryway. I felt my heart speed up. How could he do that just by holding my hand? I didn't turn around to look him in the face and try to find out what hand-holding meant. Maybe the party invitation had been enough. Maybe he had taken it as my way of saying that I'd decided to drop Jared and was interested in going out with him again.

Or maybe it meant nothing. Whatever his motivation, his hand felt good around mine. We paused a moment to let someone pass in front of us. Rob stopped quickly directly behind me and leaned against me. I could feel his breath on my neck. I wanted to turn around into his arms and tell him how much I'd missed him; tell him that I wanted to go with him to the senior prom, which he probably hadn't even thought about yet; tell him I wanted to be the girl he came home from college to see on weekends.

Instead, after the couple passed in front of us, I continued to weave through the crowd until I got to those standing and sitting in the center of the room.

Jared was among the group. I could tell from the look on his face that Rob caught Jared's name. He dropped my hand.

"How about some pizza?" I asked, trying to pretend I hadn't noticed. "We've got gobs of it in the kitchen. Any kind you've ever seen on any menu anywhere. It's build your own."

"Sounds good," he said without much conviction.

We turned and headed for the kitchen. Carmen appeared in our path. "The guest list is looking better all the time," she said to me, not taking her eyes off Rob.

"This is Rob Cantrell . . . Carmen Baedahl." I started to add "Jared's date," but decided that would sound a little obvious. I'd make my point about Jared having a date with Carmen when Carmen was safely out of earshot.

"Do you always make late dramatic entrances?" Carmen smiled up at Rob.

"Well, I try to," Rob flushed. "I need all the attention I can get."

"I doubt that," she said coyly.

I stood there like part of the furniture.

"You're not on the Brimble council, are you?" Rob said. I wondered if he thought she looked as old and sophisticated as I'd calculated earlier.

"No, not hardly," Carmen said. "I don't really have time for that sort of thing." She said it in a way that made you wonder what sort of thing she did have time for. She leaned a little closer and sipped a long swallow of Coke without taking her eyes off Rob. Then she turned back to me. "Say, you don't have anything stronger than a Coke, do you? Maybe Robbie could get me something else from the kitchen?"

"It's Rob," he corrected.

"Uh, no. Soft drinks are it," I answered.

"Maybe later, then," she cooed toward Rob with a wink and glided off toward Tim Lacey again.

Rob followed me on toward the kitchen, then said, "I really don't care for any," just as we walked up to the breakfast bar where Mary had placed a hot pineapple and Canadian-bacon pizza from the oven.

"No pizza? You don't like this kind? Mary's got more."

He grinned halfheartedly. "No, that's not it. I . . . I really have to be going."

"You just got here." I glanced at his watch. He hadn't been in the house longer than fifteen minutes.

He looked at me with a sardonic grin and whispered under his breath, "Well, I wouldn't want to let Carmen's invitation get cold."

"She'd probably wait for you."

He just wagged his head and grinned again. "But I do have to go. Really. I have another cheerleader poster party to make."

"You have to go to all of them?"

"I don't *have* to, but several asked me to come by. I hate not to show up, as council president."

I almost blurted out how egotistical I thought that idea was. Who did he think he was, the president of the United States? Was he going to bestow his blessings by giving each candidate a little crumb of his attention?

I hoped my anger didn't show. I'd accepted our first date knowing full well that half the girls in school, including Kathi, were ape over him. Knowing that he had activities competing for his time hadn't lessened his appeal, either. Dating him had almost become a challenge. Well, I wished we'd never had that first date. Then I wouldn't have known how sensitive and warm and caring he really was, under that facade. I could have continued to think he was a superficial big shot with nothing beneath the veneer. But I knew better now. I liked him and wanted him to like me, to ask me out again.

He headed for the door. "I guess I'll see you Monday."

"Okay." I willed myself to come up with something more, to tell him how I felt, to explain why I'd invited him to the party. To mention Jared and his *date*, Carmen. Rob hadn't even been around long enough for me to make that point. How stupid of me! He'd probably walked away thinking Jared was my date!

But it was too late; he was already halfway down the sidewalk. I started to close the door, and then I noticed it.

Yanking the door back open for a better look, I yelled, "My car! Look at my car!"

Rob's mouth fell open as he turned to see it. Several kids crowded into the doorway and followed me out. All four tires were slashed. Cans hung in bunches, tied to the axle. The light blue body had been spray painted with black squiggles and swirls.

chapter eleven

The estimate was $1600. The police held out little hope that they'd find who did the damage. Of course, Kathi and Melinda came immediately to my mind, but I couldn't see them personally getting their hands dirty. That's why I answered reluctantly when the investigator asked about a motive. Mother came forward with the names and addresses of both girls and filled the police in on the suspension episode.

Although she didn't come out and say it, I couldn't help but feel that Mother blamed me for the damage. Maybe if I weren't such a wimp, if I'd had more fortitude and fought back about the vodka lie, Kathi and Melinda might have let the matter drop. Although I knew they'd have sworn revenge on the Mafia itself, my mother didn't. To her, with the right approach, they could have been "taken down a couple of notches." I just hadn't been assertive enough to take care of things.

After all the kids left, Mother really lost control about the car and the whole issue of my inability to stand up for myself.

"People will run all over you if you lie down and take it," she snapped.

"What am I supposed to do?" My voice gradually rose to the same pitch as hers. "Hire a guard to watch the place when I'm gone? Even that wouldn't have helped—they had enough nerve to do it while a party was going on inside. Anybody could have walked out and caught them! Does that sound like they're easily intimidated? Does it?"

"Have you ever said one word to them since they lied about the vodka and almost got you suspended? And the egging? One word to let them know you weren't going to stand for this?"

I thought about the day at the lockers. "No, I haven't! I bow down and kiss the ground every time they walk by!"

"You'd better hold your. . . ."

"What did you want me to say to them? That I have no control over my mother? That she's the neighborhood gossip?"

"That's enough, Leanne!" Her jaw tightened, and her eyes grew bigger and black.

I could tell that I'd said more than enough. We hadn't brought up the issue of her making the phone call since the week it happened, both of us having retreated into self-righteous silence. She'd decided that she'd raised a coward for a daughter; I'd decided that I had an interfering busybody for a mother. But neither of us had expressed our disappointment in words. Now it was all coming out, and not the way I wanted it to.

In her I-told-you-so tone, she mumbled, "So this is the way a Christian young woman talks to her mother, is it?"

I swallowed hard and held my tongue. Frustration, anger, embarrassment, and regret—all four emotions washed over me. I'd never convince her that my faith made a difference, if I indulged in shouting matches with her. I stood there, trying to decide if I should apologize when I certainly didn't feel like it.

In a quieter, even disappointed tone, she finally said, "I think you should pay for half of the damage, don't you?"

"How much will it be?"

"I don't know. We've got insurance, but there's the deductible. Two hundred fifty. Something like that."

"Two hundred fifty?"

"You can pay it back when you get a job this summer. You did say you wanted to look for something, didn't you?"

I nodded and left the room. Certainly, it wasn't fair for her to have to pay for the damage, but neither should I have to. Back in my own room, I could almost see Kathi and Melinda celebrating the destruction. I had no idea who they'd talked into doing the actual tire slashing and spray painting for them, but there were guys sappy enough to do anything a girl like Kathi asked them.

If she won the cheerleading elections, it would be obvious that boys had less sense that I gave them credit for. Tina's suggestion about rigging the election came to mind. I could please Mother and give Kathi what she deserved, all with one sleight of hand, if I had the backbone, and that was a big *if*.

I was tempted. Really tempted. God, wasn't anything fair?

Finally falling asleep, I dreamed about Rob dropping by the various parties and flirting with all the candidates, wishing them all good luck—impartially, of course.

On Saturday, Philip and Mother went to buy new tires so we could drive the car to the body shop for repainting. I volunteered to go along for moral support. All three of us sat in the front seat of Philip's car in silence.

When we got home, I called Jared a couple of times, to see how things went with Carmen. The housekeeper said he wasn't staying around much anymore. What did that mean?

To top off the weekend, the police reported that when they'd questioned Kathi and Melinda, both had had alibis. Both had been at Kathi's poster party all evening with ten to twelve witnesses. So what else was new?

When I woke up Saturday morning, I wasn't sure that I could endure the coming week of campaign rhetoric—or basketball, for that matter. We were into the finals. Even though Rob had continued to attend the games, I'd made a conscious effort to block out any thoughts of him. Only after the ball had dropped through the net did I allow myself to wonder if he'd seen the shot. There was one game to go on Wednesday night, the finals. At least I had basketball to occupy my thinking, but I knew anger messed up my game, so I had to work it off before Monday's practice. But everytime I passed a store window and saw a reflection of the black swirls on my car, my stomach knotted up again.

The Sunday afternoon after the party, Rob called.

"Listen, uh. . . ." His stammering was out of character. "I just wanted to come over for a few minutes. I want to apologize about Friday night."

"You don't owe me an apology."

"Can I come over anyway?"

"I guess so."

After he hung up, I stood holding the phone. *Apologize*? The way he'd dropped my hand immediately after being introduced to Jared, I figured I'd blown everything between us. Maybe he'd realized how immature he was being. I didn't like being a pushover, but there was no denying that I was more than willing to accept his apology.

I looked at myself in the mirror. *Yuk*. My makeup had practically slidden off my face with the sweat. I'd been out on the patio, dribbling, and unintentionally knocking over plants.

Mother phoned to say that she and Philip were going out for a late lunch before coming home. "So what are you huffing and puffing about? You sound like you just ran twenty laps."

"I was dribbling out in the back."

"Why don't you channel some of that energy where it'd do some good?"

I didn't answer because she didn't expect one. What she meant was, why didn't I do something to put Kathi and Melinda in their places? Wherever that was.

After a quick shower, I put on jeans and a cinnamon-colored blouse. My hair was still French braided, and I decided to leave it alone. A touch of perfume, and I was ready when the doorbell rang. Oh, no—magazines were all over the floor where the basketball had rolled into them and started a slide. After I restacked them and finally pulled open the door, I found Rob leaning against the doorjamb, both hands tucked into his pockets.

"Nice afternoon for a nap," he said, lifting his head away from the doorframe.

"Come on, I wasn't that slow."

"I was just practicing a few putts on the green here. I'm already on the ninth hole."

"You play golf? I thought you were a diver." I was impressed. Golf seemed a sophisticated game for a high schooler.

"My dad's been taking me along with him ever since I was a little kid. He used to bore me by talking about the game; now I bore him."

"Are you any good?"

"What kind of question is that?" He pretended to take offense. "All there is to it is keeping your eye on the ball, getting a mental picture of somebody you'd like to slaughter, and then following through on a real, solid swing."

I shut the door behind me and stepped out on the sidewalk.

"You want to walk somewhere?" he asked.

"Yeah, we could walk down to the park, I guess. The end of the next block."

"I see you got new tires," he said as we passed the car that sat in the driveway announcing to the whole neighborhood that someone didn't like me—a lot.

"We got 'em yesterday. At least we can drive it now. It's a good thing Mother works close by and doesn't need it for business."

"I can just see her taking a client to lunch in it." Rob lifted his eyebrows.

"She's a prof at the college," I reminded him. "She has students, not clients."

"Right."

Another reminder about the kind of family Rob came from. Three-martini lunches, as the media referred to them, were probably something his father scheduled every day.

Who did my mother take to lunch? Perhaps students invited her to the SUB to talk her into an *A*. Then I smiled at the thought of anybody talking Mother into anything against her will.

That reminded me of Rob's scholarships. I asked if he'd heard from anywhere yet. He hadn't, but I had every confidence he would. I wondered how often he was going to come home on weekends next fall. We walked along in silence until we reached the end of the block.

"I told you on the phone that I came to apologize, and I haven't done it yet. I'm sorry about what happened to your car."

I glanced up at him. At first, I thought he was claiming responsibility for the damage. Then he said, "It's a shame the school doesn't have some way to deal with school-related vandalism. An anonymous information-reporting system, or something."

I shrugged.

"I've thought about it, but that's all. I haven't *done* anything about it. I was too busy on important things, like Who's Who in the yearbook." He kicked a rock off the sidewalk, looking pretty disgusted with himself.

So I said, "It's okay. The council can't do everything that needs doing around school."

"Just the same, I'm sorry."

I nodded.

"Did you get an estimate yet?"

"Sixteen hundred dollars."

He let out a long, low whistle.

"I don't think the police can ever do anything about it." I added, "Finding out who did it, I mean."

"Probably not."

The park looked deserted. I walked toward the swings, and Rob followed me.

"You have any idea who did it?" he asked.

I caught myself before the accusations came out. I had seen Kathi talking to him several times in the hall, and he'd probably been to her poster party Friday night. "I think I know, but I'd rather not say until I'm sure."

"Kathi and Melinda?" he prodded.

I sat down in the swing and turned my face away from him. Did he still like Kathi? Had he been dating her again? Was he just trying to weasel information out of me? He stepped behind me and gave me a push.

"What do you think?" I asked.

"Probably. But not personally."

"Do you know who did it, or are you just guessing?"

"Guessing. I went by Kathi's poster party at Melinda's after I left here the other night."

I noted the order of his agenda. Maybe he would have skipped Kathi's party altogether, if I hadn't been so insensitive as to force him to confront Jared. And he still didn't know Jared had had a date with someone else. How could I bring that up now?

He continued his explanation as he absentmindedly pushed my swing forward each time it returned. "About fifteen minutes after I got there, a car full of four or five guys drove up and talked to Kathi. They never came inside the garage. Everybody was outside in the garage with the posters spread around, so we could see what everybody else was doing."

So that's how the successful party givers did it. In the garage? Well, it certainly was more relaxed for sure.

Rob gave me another push. "Kathi and Melinda walked out to

the street to talk to them. I couldn't see everyone in the car, but Wade Abdulker was one of them, and so was Rudy Curbow."

"You think that's who Kathi got to do it?"

"Maybe. But they're not exactly her style."

I wondered what he meant by that, but he clarified without my asking.

"She's not in that kind of crowd, normally. She's a good kid." His terminology surprised me; he sounded like a graduate student assessing the friend of his little sis. Although I didn't agree with his judgment, I knew what he meant: Kathi wasn't on drugs, wasn't a truant, wasn't a dropout. She was just your average, vindictive, middle-class student.

But on second thought, maybe he meant more. Maybe he thought that just because she dressed like a millionaire and had a hotshot lawyer father, that made her a good kid. Boys were so stupid sometimes. They couldn't see in front of their noses. It wouldn't have surprised me at all if Kathi were elected cheerleader by the male vote alone.

"Do the good kids always get somebody else to do their dirty work for them?" I asked, not bothering to curb my sarcasm.

"I don't know. I didn't say Kathi did it. I just said they were kind of loud and thought something was awfully funny," he continued, completely oblivious to the bitterness I felt. "Kathi and Melinda came back to the garage where the rest of us were, and the carload of guys drove off."

He pushed me a little higher in the swing. Then he added, "But thinking about the way they were whispering and some of the cracks they made after they came back into the garage helped me put two and two together."

"Comments like what?" I probed.

"Like what was her favorite color for a car? Things like that. Nothing really incriminating, but . . ." his voice trailed off.

I dragged my foot to stop the swing, got off, walked over to a shade tree, and sat down in the grass. Rob dropped down in front of me. Then he moved over with his back to the tree trunk and propped himself up to face me for a long moment.

"I'm sorry about what happened, anyway." He leaned up, took me in his arms, and kissed me gently. We sat looking at each other for a long time.

"You're what I've been waiting for, you know that?" he asked.

"I'm glad you waited."

"I can't believe I feel like this after only one date."

"And after an awful lot of student council meetings," I added.

He pulled my chin up so that I looked him straight in the eyes. "You know what my dad said when he saw your picture in the yearbook?"

"That I'd make a good caddy?" I teased.

"Exactly."

I swatted at his face, and he ducked.

"He said, 'She's good-looking, too.' "

"And that surprises you?" I pretended to be hurt.

"No," he looked sheepish. "Somehow that lost something in the translation."

I smiled and waited.

"You see, on the golf course, we get into serious discussions sometimes. We're always teasing each other about who we rate as tens."

"You mean there are that many tens around?"

"That's just the point. There are only a lot in my dad's eyes. I'm more particular than he is. A girl's got to have some brains, to my way of thinking. Can you see a Brenda Andrus giving medicine to a sick child? She probably has trouble telling the difference between a tablespoon and a teaspoon. I don't think she's taken too many higher math courses."

"You're terrible."

"Nothing personal. Just a type."

I acted offended for all the klutzy Brenda Andruses of the world. Her clumsiness wasn't her fault.

"But back to the issue," he said. "Besides having brains and beauty, a woman has to know who she is. She needs poise and all that good stuff. I don't want somebody who hasn't got the self-confidence to be herself and operate on her own value system."

I nodded. I'd been right all along. Rob's ego thing was all an act. He really did care about important things. He and Jared *were* alike, just as I thought.

"Anyway, like I was saying. My dad knows what my requirements are in women, and he knows that's why I don't . . . well, why I haven't dated many girls seriously. That is, more than once or twice. It doesn't take me long to find a missing part to their puzzle."

Did I dare? I decided to chance it. "So now I know why you haven't asked me out again."

Evidently he didn't catch the line. He seemed to move into another mood altogether, dropped his arms, and leaned back against the tree trunk again. I regretted having broken the spell.

"You still see Jared?"

I didn't know how to answer. The way he'd phrased the question made it seem like we were "seeing" each other as in dating. Of course, we'd been together even more in the last two weeks, planning the party. But we hadn't been to a movie in a couple of months.

"I see him some, yes. We ride horses together."

"I guess guys like him need some kind of calling."

I was offended for real this time. "I don't know what you mean about 'guys like him.' "

Rob shrugged. "I didn't know girls went for his type."

"What type?" I grew more defensive by the second. Pulling my shoulders up straighter, I faced him.

"You know: quiet, small for his age."

"How do you know he's quiet? You didn't stay long enough the other night to notice."

"Just the look in his eye says he's shy. And you said you went out to talk to him at the basketball game because he didn't have any friends and wouldn't come inside."

"He could have all the friends he wanted! He just needs a little self-confidence. Not everybody can be student council president." I knew that remark would hurt him. On our first date we'd discussed vanity and shallowness. I'd even told him I once thought he was like that, until I got to know him and saw he was sincere.

Rob stood up; I did likewise. I couldn't tell if he was planning to end the conversation or not. We held each other's gaze for a long time. At first his eyes were angry, then they softened.

"Like I said, let me know when you and Jared call it quits."

"If you had stayed around long enough the other night, you'd have found out that Jared had a date with Carmen!" I paused to let that soak in. "Jared is a good friend of mine, and I intend to keep it that way. He's like the brother I never had."

"*Brothers* in that sense frequently turn out to be something more," he said coolly.

I didn't respond but thought of the summer morning Jared had kissed me and told me how he felt about me.

"Running into exboyfriends everytime I come around here could get a little odd."

"Jared is a *friend*," I repeated firmly, surprising myself by the level, matter-of-fact tone I'd managed. Did he realize how inconsistent he sounded? Which was the real Rob? Did he want a girl whom he could persuade to drop an old friend for no reason? Or did he really want a girl with convictions and a mind of her own?

"Sounds like you're together until death do you part, if you ask me."

"Can't you understand a friendship with someone of the opposite sex?"

"Yes, I can understand just being friends," he replied. "But I think *you're* the one who's confused."

"About what?"

"About what you feel. Jared's still your first priority. Whenever he snaps his fingers—just like at the ballgame when you sneaked out—you'll come running. No matter when or where or who you're with."

"You went to Kathi's party, didn't you?"

"That's different."

"How?"

"She's not a friend. She's a candidate who asked me to come by, just like all the others did, because I was council president." He turned abruptly and walked toward the street.

"Rob?"

He turned around, waited.

"Nothing," I said finally.

"You want me to walk you back to your house?" he asked levelly.

"It's broad daylight. I think I can manage."

He headed for the street again.

My mother would have been proud.

chapter twelve

Matt "the Man" Corley literally ran into me as I was leaving the building after basketball practice. He sometimes came by after school and jogged around the football track.

"Who else did you sweep off their feet today?" he asked me.

"Sorry. I'll honk next time I approach a corner."

"Got a minute? I was just jogging inside for a drink of water."

I nodded, turned around, and followed him back inside the gym.

"What do you hear about All-District?" he asked, still puffing slightly.

"I'm still in the running, I guess. The benching hurt me, though."

"Hey, you're too young, anyway. You'd give all those senior forwards at Peoria a complex."

"Sure, it'd be really big of me to let one of them win this year. I'll remember it as my good deed."

He bent down to gulp from the fountain, and I waited. "So what else is new?" he asked as he straightened up again and we started back outside.

"Well, let's see. Besides almost being suspended and really being benched, having my house egged, one mysterious locker episode, and my car's new paint job, I guess nothing much is happening."

Matt wiped his long, sweaty arm across his forehead and grinned. "Well, glad to hear everything's going just fine during the proverbial best years of your life."

"Yeah. Sure. Fine." I rolled my eyes at him.

"You and Jared still friends?"

"Yes. That's the problem."

"Well now, that's a new twist. When friends start causing problems, it's time to trade them in for enemies."

I told him about my one and only date with Rob and how he felt about my friendship with Jared.

"Well, if he's going to be that way about it, I'd tell Mr. Wonderful to cool it about your other friends. Particularly since he himself is a newcomer to the list."

"But I can see his point," I argued against my own former position. "He doesn't want to waste time getting to know a girl who's interested in someone else. He says he's waited a long time for the right girl to come along and if it's the real thing, he expects her to feel the same way. Or, at least, to give it a good chance."

"Well, you certainly might feel the same way—given a little more time, that is. But I think he's got the cart before the horse. There's a lot of liking that's got to come before loving."

I thought that over. I'd never seriously used the word *love* with a boyfriend. Of course, I probably did when I was a child of seven or eight, but that was different. I was sixteen, Rob was eighteen; we were both old enough to use the word sparingly. It wasn't that I really thought so lightly of real love—the marrying kind. In fact, I'd given it a lot of thought, especially since Mother and Dad split up. I guess you could say I had discussed, defined, redefined, and defended it a good deal with Tina. I was trying to look at everything in a new light since the divorce, and since I'd become a Christian. But it wasn't easy, especially when applying the Christian definition of *love* to a person as spiteful as Kathi.

Matt stood staring at me, hands on his hips, perspiration pouring off his face, neck, and arms. His beard, although neatly trimmed, and his large six-foot-six frame gave him a rugged look and explained why the kids around school had begun calling him Matt the Man. Considering his size, I still felt petite around him; and his physical size had a psychological effect, too. He came across wiser, if you know what I mean. All the kids at church respected his opinion about things because he lived what he taught, without having to preach it. Hanging around campus two or three days a week, he'd made quite a few friendships with some of the school leaders and athletes, hoping to give them some support in their leadership decisions that affected morals. In short, most everybody liked him; he was sort of like an unofficial "counselor at large."

"What does your mother say?" He brought me back to the point.

"She says I've given Jared all the help called for. The old 'God helps them that help themselves' philosophy."

"Not too biblical, is it? By the way, how are your mother's TA salary negotiations coming along?"

"Not too well. They staged a one-day walkout, but it wasn't too effective. The students all got walks, and the TAs made their point, but their salaries are still the same."

"I don't imagine your mom's too popular at the moment with the administration, then?"

"Not exactly."

"Which goes to show you, I guess, that might doesn't always make right, huh?"

"I don't know about that. Kathi and Melinda seem to be doing something right. They got their folks to get them permission to take the exams they missed during suspension. Now she's eligible for cheerleader, and I won't be surprised if she wins."

"Don't lose perspective. Remember, in the profound words of that immortal, great philosopher Yogi Berra, 'It's not over till it's over.' "

I grinned. Matt was always quoting some athlete's nonsensical mumblings from after-game TV interviews.

"Or to put it in operatic terms," he continued, "it's not over till the fat lady sings."

"Get me a piano, then."

He laughed. "If I've gotten a correct handle on Rob this last year while I've been hanging around campus, I'd say it won't hurt him to swallow a little pride. He knows a good woman when he sees one. He'll come around. If he doesn't, he's not worth your time."

"How about Kathi? Is she worth my time? I'd like to spend a few hours making her life as miserable as she's made mine."

"No way," Matt shook his head at me with a big, broad smile. "Forget that. Forget about what she's up to. That's a Matt Corley translation of 'Vengeance is mine, saith the Lord.' "

I shrugged. He turned and started to jog off again. "Call me again if I can help. You know, talk to Jared again."

"Sure." Then I called after him, "But it's his dad who needs the help."

His voice trailed further away, "Well, let me know. I think I still speak adult well enough to get through to him, too."

I waved him on around the track and headed home myself.

Seeing Kathi's posters on every empty wall space the week of cheerleader elections revolted me. We'd had the car repainted, and I'd talked to the manager of the bookstore in the mall about a summer job. He said he could use me about sixteen hours a week as vacation relief for the regular employees. Using the first $250 I would earn to pay the deductible on the car didn't set well yet.

I had phoned Jared at least once a day for the whole week, but still hadn't talked to him since the party. I caught the housekeeper once more before she left for the evening, but she was vague about why Jared couldn't come to the phone. Maybe he was spending a lot of time with Carmen? Hadn't I gotten through to him at all and convinced him that he was a worthwhile person who could make friends if he tried? Why hadn't he returned any of my phone calls? What was with him, anyway? Was this friendship really worth the effort?

Rob also became a taboo subject, even with Tina. We'd discussed him until we had each other's arguments memorized. She couldn't see what the big deal was. Rob wanted Jared out of the picture, so *get* Jared out of the picture.

Mother agreed. Not that she was not all for "charity," she said, but enough was enough. Jared had proven himself hopeless, "a rich-kid misfit who had suicidal tendencies," she'd summarily labeled him.

I didn't agree, but I no longer argued.

"Today's the big day," Tina said when we met in second period. I lifted the corner of my mouth, as in "What big day?"

"Elections."

"Oh, I thought you meant. . . ." I never finished. Nobody was as interested in All-District as I was, not even Tina. At least I knew Jared cared. That is, I thought he did. I decided he must be living with the horses.

"Cheerleader elections." Tina eyed me with a mischievous grin. "As in vote counting. Remember?"

I didn't share her enthusiasm about the suggestion she'd made earlier. However, when I thought about the car, the idea grew more tempting than when I'd had only the Vodka Caper and egging to contend with.

But the chances that I'd be helping to count votes were slim—one in twenty, to be exact. There were twenty office aides. Anything other than picking up absentee cards, marking the records, and dispensing messages to the teachers' boxes was after-school duty. Usually Ms. Welsh, the attendance clerk who supervised the office aides, asked for volunteers during the day. Most only volunteered to stay for after-school tasks when they were put on the spot, but counting cheerleading votes would be different; several would probably volunteer for that job.

"I don't think so," I reaffirmed to myself as well as to Tina. "I don't think I could do it."

"After what they did?" Tina sounded incredulous. "They got off scot-free with everything. No zeros! No ineligibility! No car repair bill! No police record! All they got was a nice five-day vacation and a lot of publicity, which will probably help elect Kathi cheerleader."

"Shhhh," I said. Everybody was still talking while Mrs. Wolenhueter called roll, but Tina's voice carried when she got excited or angry or both.

"And all *you* got was a chance to give away two weeks' salary this summer to pay for the repaint job. You know, I'm beginning to believe your mother's right! You'd let anybody stomp on you and then kiss the bottom of their feet!"

"You know, for someone with a twenty-two-inch waist, you sure do have a big mouth."

"You just wait. Kathi's going to get you yet. You just wait and see if I'm not right. I can't believe you." Tina harumphed and shifted her position to let me know she was through with her pep talk and the results were totally in my hands.

Maybe this was God's way of helping me even the score? Maybe He'd see that I got to count the votes. But I knew better. Still, it was a thought.

When fourth period came and Ms. Welsh asked if anybody wanted to stay after school to count votes, I volunteered.

chapter thirteen

The packed gym roared with kids laughing and shouting to one another from opposite sides. The teachers on duty sauntered around as if oblivious to all of it. Someone in the sophomore section cupped his hands around his mouth and shouted, "Freshmen, why don't you go home and take a nap? We need more room in here."

Laughter came from those seated around him. The freshmen booed.

The last few classes came through the doors and wandered up and down the bleachers trying to find places to squeeze in. Cheerleader tryouts weren't that big an event to the majority of students, but the alternative was study hall, so most of the school was packing itself into the gym, which wasn't meant to handle that many people.

Tina leaned closer to me. "If you have a chance, you can miss a few votes for Deidra Hartman, too."

"Who's she?"

"In the second group of sophomores." Tina pointed her out.

"What did she do to you?"

"Nothing. I just think she's stuck-up."

Tina seemed to be so sure about how simple it would be to "miss a few votes," as she put it.

"Look, I don't think. . . ."

"Have you lost your nerve again?"

I didn't answer. *Again*? I'd never agreed in the first place. I'd simply volunteered to stay after school to help.

"It'll be so simple," she continued. "Somebody'll be calling the votes out to you, and you'll record them. You just won't mark down a few—or a lot, depending. Haven't you seen the ballots?"

I hadn't. Tina continued, "I bet they're just like last year's. All the names will be listed, and we circle three out of eight. Whoever calls them to you won't be paying attention to your marking."

"Are we going to vote in here?" I changed the subject. "How will they keep juniors from voting for sophomores and sophomores from taking freshmen ballots?"

"We'll get the ballots when we go back to homeroom after this. Sophomore homerooms only get sophomore ballots."

I began to feel a little dense because I couldn't remember the way it was done last year. A psychological block? A warning?

"There's no way they'll know how many really voted. Some kids don't even care enough to mark a ballot. And some only circle one name if they don't know anybody else who's listed. There's no way Ms. Welsh could know how many total votes there should be, unless somebody got two thousand votes when we only have seven hundred sophomores. But you're going to be subtracting, not adding."

I didn't argue. I turned back to watch Rob as he plugged in the microphones and said, "Testing . . . one, two, three." My palms felt sweaty, like they did sometimes when we were in the final moments of a close game. But now I knew why. Watching Kathi as she stood at the bottom of the bleachers waving to different kids almost made me physically sick. I'd never been jealous, and that's not how I would have labeled my feelings at the present. What I really felt was pure disgust, the kind of attitude Mother always said would only ruin my game. Well, the season was over!

Kathi stepped up onto the second row of the bleachers and leaned over Mike Plummel, pretending to be reaching for something in her friend's purse behind him. Mike and the guy on the other side kept winking and daring each other to pinch her. Then Mike did, and Kathi squealed and slapped him, making a fuss loud enough so that everybody around was sure to notice what happened. I watched all this and loathed what I was thinking as much as I did Kathi. Maybe I'd turn into some kind of cat.

But then Tina's reasoning hit me again. I visualized the car the night of the party and Kathi's triumphant smile outside the principal's office. But for sheer luck, the day at the lockers could have been added to the list of injuries. What was the worst they could have done? Planted marijuana or crack? I thought of how the kids from Brimble had looked at me and the car that night. I know they felt sorry for me about the damage, but I couldn't help but wonder if they thought I might have deserved it. If no one had known, it would have been easier to try to forget and forgive it. But everyone knew. That was the thing. Everyone knew, including Mother. So what was I going to do about it?

Rob picked up the microphone and called for everyone's attention, to explain how we would handle the tryouts. Only the freshmen listened.

"At least we don't have to sit through too many," Tina said. "I'm sure glad the teachers eliminated the duds. Not that they couldn't have eliminated a few more. I've got a mirror; you'd think some of them would too."

I smirked. Tina wasn't that unattractive; she was just average. Besides having a perfect figure from her weight-lifting exercises, she had a good smile.

The group of eight freshmen took the floor and began their first of two yells. I spotted who I thought would be elected: the two on the far end. They shouted at the top of their lungs, but the rest of them were too concerned with the movements. "The two on the end should get it. They're good," I said to Tina.

"But you know freshmen. The rest of the class probably doesn't have the sense to pick them out."

I ignored her. I tried not to pull too much of that upperclass stuff myself, because reps from all grade levels have to work together on the council. Too much upperclass snobbishness could make for a very long year.

The freshmen candidates led one more yell and then were individually introduced. They wore numbers, but Rob called their names, anyway. "Here on the far corner is Laurel . . . Hardy. No, no, sorry about that." He grinned, and she giggled. "Laurel Odelemeyer." He messed up the pronunciation and corrected himself. "That's a tongue twister. Did your parents know they were doing that to you?" She nodded yes.

He moved on to the next girl. "This is Susan Vassal. Blond hair down—let's see—two inches below the shoulders. Note that on your ballot; it might make a difference. You need to be able to distinguish her from the next name," he moved on to the third candidate, "which is Susan Graham, who has blond hair . . . turn around . . . about four inches below the shoulder, right? Watch that carefully, freshmen. Got that difference? Two inches versus four inches."

The two girls looked nothing alike.

I listened as Rob continued the introductions. The candidates ate up their time in the limelight. Some of them who would lose this election wouldn't have the nerve to go out for anything again. I know I wouldn't.

After the last freshman was introduced, the sophomore group took the court and spread themselves out the length of the gym. They did their two short yells quickly, which was a good thing, because by the time the juniors got up, everyone was getting restless.

Kathi, a junior, was up next. During the yells, Rob always took a seat on the bottom row of the bleachers on the opposite side of the gym from Tina and me. I held my head in the direction of Sharon Slade, whom I hoped would win. I could feel Rob's eyes on me. What was he thinking?

For a moment, I entertained the idea that Mother and Kathi were alike. But on second thought, there was a big difference. Even though they both knew how to get what they wanted, they wanted different things. Mother used her assertiveness on worthwhile things like getting TAs a decent wage. Kathi used her charms for things like hair codes and slashed car tires.

With my head angled toward Sharon Slade, I let my eyes rove to the other candidates and finally rest again on Rob. Being seated on the opposite side of the gym, he couldn't see exactly where I was looking, but I could tell he was looking in my direction. Some freshmen girls who were seated near him were leaning over and talking to him. "Entertaining the troops," I'd teased him one day about the girls that hung around him all the time. If they only knew that he was so different from the image he projected—more serious, sensitive. Wasn't he? Did I know the real Rob, or had I been duped like the rest?

The juniors finished, and Rob introduced them individually. When he got to Kathi, he said, "Kathi Ross, as in Who's Who in hair codes." I felt sure he did that for Tim Lacey's benefit.

But then I wondered if Rob's reference to the hair-code episode, even if it was the first thing that came to his mind, had real meaning. Maybe he did admire Kathi for her determination to get what she wanted. He'd told me he wanted a girl who operated out of her own value system. Maybe he was talking about someone with the strength to buck whatever everybody else thought. Well, if that's what he meant about *values,* and Kathi filled the bill, I was out in left field.

Tina's ballot-counting suggestion flashed into my mind again. I wondered if Rob would label that gutsy.

When the juniors finished, Rob took the mike again and gave the teachers and students final instructions about marking ballots, which had been placed in the homeroom teachers' boxes. Classes were to mark the ballots immediately and send them to Ms. Welsh in the office.

As soon as he dismissed everybody, kids stampeded through the gym doors. It was always unbearably hot in the gym with that many bodies packed in. The seniors hung around, taking their time about getting back to class, because they had no ballots to mark.

As Tina and I inched along with the crowd, I kept an eye on Rob and the two senior girls talking to him. As they moved on, he wandered over to the candidates, who were being hugged by three outgoing senior cheerleaders.

As the crowd moved Tina and me along to the doorway and freedom, someone pushed us from behind. I glanced over my shoulder and saw Kathi and three other candidates excusing their way through the crowd.

Tina interpreted to me. "Excuse us, as in move over, world, Kathi Ross wants through."

Kathi wiggled her way through to where Tina and I stood blocked in. Then she edged around us without so much as a word, only a look, as if she were surveying the downtrodden masses meant to be her audience.

"Good luck, Kathiiiii," one of her friends waved to her over the crowd of pushing shoulders.

"After a suspension" she cut her eyes in our direction, "made me miss gymnastic practice for a week, I'll need it."

"Oh, no, you'll win," her friend assured her.

At the gym door, Tina and I squeezed through at the same time. Tina, with her conspiratorial look, said, "Call me as soon as you get home." She turned into the east wing; I headed for the west wing. One good thing about Herrington: You always got lots of exercise, just hiking from class to class.

During fifth period, I tried to table the ideas swimming through my head. When the situation floated into my consciousness, I promised myself I'd think about it later. Tina had sounded so sure. But I might not even get the junior ballots to count. If I did count them, I might not be doing the marking. It was easier not to think about it. When the time came, I'd do what I had to do.

The time came.

Ms. Welsh sent the regular sixth-period aides around to get the attendance cards from each classroom, then she took care of the two kids hanging over the front counter in the office, waiting to sign out for the day. One was giving her a story about a dental appointment that didn't jibe with the time his mother had mentioned in her early-release note. After he signed out, the second student asked if anybody had turned in his algebra book. She checked the lost and found and handed him the book. He walked out without even thanking her. That's one thing I always hated about working in the office: Some of the students were so obnoxious.

Ms. Welsh turned to the three of us waiting to count ballots. "Okay, girls, this way." She led us into her glass cubicle and handed over the ballots. I swallowed hard when I saw some junior ballots in my pile.

"I've given each of you a third of the ballots from all of the classes." She handed us each clean ballots where we were to mark lines beside the names to indicate each vote. "That way, nobody will know the final numbers until you turn all three master ballots in to me."

"Oh, rats," Misty said. "That was the reason I volunteered to count. I wanted to know who was going to get it."

Ms. Welsh grinned. "Sorry about that, but that's the idea."

Each of us shuffled around until we found an empty spot.

"All right, go to it," she said.

I turned my back to the others and began work.

chapter fourteen

"Jared, it's me. I'm coming over."

"Look, wait. My dad and I . . . well, we had this big fight, and I don't feel like. . . ."

"I don't care. I'm coming anyway."

His voice had sounded strange and faraway, like it had the night of the gym conversation. I didn't intend to prod him about that; I wanted to unload on *him* this time. I was tired of Tina and Rob and Kathi and Mother and everybody else. I kept the car window down and let the wind whip me in the face. Strands of hair flapped into my eyes from time to time. I deserved it.

On the tennis court, we didn't talk. Jared's serve was wicked. He slammed it into my court as I stood on tiptoes, leaning toward it expectantly. I missed—again, and again, and again.

After he'd taken the first two games without my getting a single point, he said, "You sure you want to play?"

I shook my head. "Why don't we just use the backboard?"

He nodded and I walked toward the far fence.

"Go ahead," he said. "I think I'm going to practice my serve."

I slammed the first ball toward the backboard as he went to the other end of the court, where his bucket of balls sat. For the next half hour we were oblivious to each other. I continued to slam first one ball and then the next against the board. I lunged to return them, as if my life depended on it—to the right, the left, overhead, forearm swing, another overhead, then backhanded. The ball sailed back and forth without respite.

With the last drop of energy drained from my body, I picked up the balls and headed toward the backyard. Jared caught up with me. "Got it out of your system?"

I nodded.

"Too bad it's not that simple for me," he mumbled so low that I almost didn't hear him.

"What?"

"Nothing." He never slowed his pace as we headed for my car.

"Thanks." I climbed in and drove home. No explanations were necessary. We were that kind of friends.

When I got home at six, Mother said Tina had called twice and wanted me to return the call the minute I walked in the door.

I sat down at the kitchen table, smelling the pineapple burgers in the oven. "I'll have it ready in a few minutes," she said. "I want to get to the library by seven."

I kept my seat at the table by way of answer.

"You look like you had a good day," she said. I glanced at her, to see if she was teasing. She was. "Want to talk about it?"

"Not really."

"Rob?"

"No."

She dropped the subject and put the food on the counter for us to fill our plates. We ate without talking.

"I'll clean up here, if you're in a hurry," I said when we'd finished. I might as well be good for something.

"The dishes can wait until I come in. You never did call Tina."

"I know."

She shrugged, picked up her books, and left for the library.

At nine, Tina phoned again, and I had to tell her I hadn't done it.

So why was I so angry with myself, if I'd done what was right? You tell me. Whoever said that if you did what was right, it'd all come out okay in the end didn't know Kathi Ross. Or Rob Cantrell. Kathi was still "riding high" as my mother would say, and Rob was still drifting away. So where was my pat on the back?

By second-period announcements the next morning, Tina had regained her perspective. She didn't refer to the vote counting and how I'd "let her down" at all. Somehow she'd taken the whole thing personally, as if the problem had been between her and Kathi. I supposed I should have felt grateful that she cared so much.

She had not even speculated about the election outcome, and I was sure that took considerable restraint on her part. I appreciated it. Instead, we discussed our assignment to read John Updike's "A&P." I loved it, which was a shock; most of the time I have to look back over the assignment, just to remember what the story was about.

"I don't see how she could give us a pop quiz on this, do you?" Tina asked. "I mean, what kind of questions could she ask? What color were the narrator's socks?"

"She doesn't look in a quiz mood. It's Friday," I said. "She wouldn't give us one today, anyway, because I remember the story." I was getting more cynical by the minute.

Tina agreed and closed her text. Rob's voice came on with the announcements. First there was the announcement about when the next SAT tests would be given for seniors who had still not taken them. Interested students were to contact the counselor "T-O-D-A-Y." Rob spelled it out, probably just as Mr. Warner had scribbled it on the slip of paper. Everybody laughed when he started spelling, because we all knew Mr. Warner and his notes.

When he sends his thousand and one notes home with us throughout the year—about available scholarships, testing, open house, graduation, summer school, parking violations—practically every other word is caps. Rob had even read two or three announcements over the intercom emphasizing each capped or underlined word. The announcements had sounded ridiculous, and Mr. Warner had taken to reading his own for the next several weeks.

"Now for the biggies," Rob was saying. Everybody got a little quieter. "Congratulations to Leanne Markwardt. She has been named All-District, and," he paused, "she has also been named to the All-State girls' basketball team. I might add, she is the first sophomore to hold that honor in the last eight years. Congratulations, Leanne, from the student body."

Everybody around me started clapping, and some said, "Speech, speech." Tina hugged me and so did Marianne Spears and Camey McQuire, who sat in front of me.

Then Frank Blumenthal turned to Mrs. Wolenhueter. "I think that calls for a celebration, don't you? We ought to dismiss the class and go out for beer."

She didn't answer him but smiled in my direction and congratulated me. Rob's voice grew louder as the comments around me subsided.

"Another biggie this morning. Good news comes all at once. Cheerleader election results." The class quieted down again.

It struck me funny that they'd really care who won. Being on the council, I heard the same comment, election after election: "Why do the same old ones get everything?" I always wanted to stand up and say, "Because you keep voting for them, that's why! Why don't you come up with some new names once in a while?" I had never had the nerve to say it, but there was nothing unusual in that.

Rob called out the freshmen winners, then waited for the

applause that could be heard from each classroom down the hall. Then he continued with the sophomore and junior winners.

Kathi's name was not called. Had they made some mistake? From the third of the ballots I'd counted, she was headed for a three-way tie.

Tina leaned over to me. "Looks like our fellow classmates have more sense than we gave them credit for."

"Looks that way."

"Let's just hope Kathi doesn't find out who counted votes."

chapter fifteen

"Nice," Tina said, walking around me to examine my new pants and blouse more carefully before we left for the movie.

"A gift to myself."

"So what's the occasion?"

I stared at her, thinking that maybe she wasn't such a good friend, after all.

"Oh, yeah. Sorry about that. Congrats again. First sophomore to make it. You should have All-State inscribed on your pockets."

Maybe that's what it'd take before anyone mentioned it again. After second period, it had been like a blackout—not a word.

I'd called Jared after school to tell him, but Mary had said he wasn't around. *Again*, I left word for him to call me. He hadn't. How much longer before he snapped out of it? And Rob's congratulations on the PA system certainly lacked the personal touch.

When we were almost to the movie, Tina remembered that she didn't have any money with her. "We've got to go back home."

"Don't turn around. You can borrow some from me."

"You don't have enough."

"How do you know? What are you going to do, buy the whole *cinema?*"

She ignored me and made a quick Louie, anyway. Twenty minutes later, I followed her back inside their apartment.

"Surprise," somebody yelled from behind me as we walked through the door. Kids began coming out of the entryway closet, the kitchen pantry, and her little sister's toy box.

"What is this?" I turned to Tina. "I didn't miss your birthday, did I?"

"No dummy. This is for you. For All-State."

I could feel my mouth gape. Then everybody kept asking me if I'd suspected anything while I assured them I hadn't. And Tina kept repeating how she lured me to the movie and how she put the party together on such short notice after second-period announcements. "We're not having much to eat," she kept saying. "I hope everybody had a big steak before they came."

"Davia Crawford!" I screamed, hugging an old friend's neck. "When did you get back? What are you doing here?"

Davia had been a really close friend of mine before she had to move away to live with her grandmother. "What happened? Why are you back?" I repeated.

Tears welled up in her eyes. "I'll tell you later." She looked away, "Congratulations."

I felt sad and glad all at once, but this wasn't the time to find out what had happened in her life during the months she'd been away. I just hugged her again, instead. Then, standing around in kind of a daze, I watched while Tina tried to herd everybody down to the apartment pool. She handed trays of sandwiches, cheese, and chips to different ones as they exited.

Rob wasn't in the lineup.

I hung around in the kitchen and tried to be useful, counting out the napkins, plates, and cups until everybody was out the door. "I hate to be a party pooper," I said to Tina, "but I don't have a suit. I noticed everybody else had theirs on under their clothes."

"Never fear," Tina pointed to the bedroom, "your mother brought yours by earlier, when she left the car for you. Didn't you see it parked around the corner?" I shook my head in amazement. "You can change in there and come on down."

"You're something else," I said.

"Don't say what," she grinned.

A couple of guys came back inside to help carry more food down as I wandered off into the bedroom.

While I rummaged around trying to find my suit, I could hear Tim Lacey. "We're going to freeze our nostrils together, aren't we?"

"No, it's heated–just for you. Stay underwater," Tina answered him. "Here, take this carton. I have the other." The door closed and everything was quiet again.

I finally found the suit, changed, and rolled up my clothes to stash in an out-of-the-way place. I didn't want somebody coming in to use the bathroom to find them lying all around. Then I decided to put my hair on top of my head—if I could find some pins in Tina's makeup drawer.

When I came back out of the bathroom into her bedroom a few minutes later, I heard Tina on the phone in the kitchen. She said Rob's name.

"I'm having a surprise party for Leanne tonight, to celebrate All-State. I've been trying all afternoon to catch you. So are you coming?" Her tone was impatient. "Who said you had to go to all the cheerleading parties? Is that in your job description?"

I felt as if I had a big coconut in the pit of my stomach.

"As a member of the council, what? Who do you think you are, God or something? This is high school, Rob Cantrell. You're not president of the United States yet. Don't worry about having to slice yourself so thin!"

I felt the tears come and closed my eyes to discourage them, but it was no use. I pulled a Kleenex out of the drawer and pressed it under each eye just below the lower lashes. At least I could save my makeup. After all, Tina had gone to lots of trouble to plan the party, and I wasn't going to let her know I cared that Rob couldn't spare the time.

"How did you mean it, then?" Tina asked coldly. "Well, are you coming or not? Good!" She hung up.

I opened the bedroom door and walked out. Tina jumped.

"Leanne." She turned pale. "I didn't know you were still in here. I thought you went down to the pool already."

There was no need for words. I shut the door behind me and came out into the kitchen. She could tell from the look on my face that I'd heard everything.

"He's coming," was what she finally said. "I should have gotten ahold of him earlier, but I couldn't catch him at school. He already had plans, but he's going to break them. He was supposed to go by one of the cheerleader's parties."

"You talked him out of it, I gather."

"Not really," Tina averted her eyes. "I didn't have to *talk him into it*, I mean. He just thought he should put in an appearance over there." She tried to make it sound obligatory for him to attend the other party.

We just stood looking at each other for a moment. I wanted to tell her that it was okay, that I was going to give up on him, anyway, but I figured she could tell from my face that that was a lie, too.

"Do you think I'm being stubborn?" I asked.

"About what?"

"About Jared. About refusing to tell Rob that I'll stop going over to Jared's and stop being his friend."

"Well." She drew out the word, then paused.

"I know you do," I answered for her, then paused, knowing she still didn't understand my stubbornness, as she referred to it. "Did you invite Jared tonight? I bet you didn't have to beg him to come, did you?"

"No, I didn't." Tina looked sheepish. "I didn't call him, that is."

I stood looking at her.

"But I will, if you want me to. You want me to? I didn't think you'd want to make the same mistake twice. Rob's going to be here later."

"Maybe. If he can work it into his schedule," I corrected her, with a large dose of sarcasm.

"Well, do you really want me to call Jared?" Tina asked.

I nodded, and she went to the phone. No answer.

"Look, I'm sorry," I said when she hung up the phone. "Don't worry about it. That's fine." I didn't want her to think I was ungrateful about all she'd done. "The party idea was really sweet. It's fine. I'm just stubborn about all the wrong things."

Tina handed me another Kleenex from the kitchen drawer.

I continued, "Somehow I manage to stand up to Rob about not ditching Jared when I shouldn't. And then I can't manage to stand up to Kathi Ross when I should. Mother said I lack a sense of self, if you know what she means by that. And Rob says I operate out of a different value system than most people." I felt I was just rattling on incoherently, but things had been bottled up inside for so long that I couldn't seem to help myself. "Am I really that weird?"

Tina stood looking at me for a long time, as if she were thinking it over. But she had on her You're-crazy-but-I-love-you-anyway grin.

"Well, am I?" I repeated, this time laughing more than crying.

"You're weird, all right." Tina knew I was over the worst now. "Give you a party and you stand in the kitchen crying."

"I'm sorry. I really am. I'm okay now, honest. Rob can hang it up. He and my mother ought to get together and compare notes. They'd think they were talking about two different people."

"Maybe they are. Like Rob said about operating on your own values—you stand firm when it's important, and you let it go when it's not. The problem is you and your mom have different ideas about what's worth fighting for."

I nodded. "Okay. Okay. I'm starting over. Rob's coming, and I'm going to give him my undivided, loving, loyal attention."

"Atta girl." She picked up the rest of the cups. "See you downstairs." She closed the door behind her, and I finished poking the last few pins in my hair before catching up to her on the stairs.

"Hey, everybody, don't go in yet. We're going to eat first," Tina yelled loud enough for the entire apartment complex to hear her. Those who had not yet sunk into the warm water gathered around the two folding tables she'd pulled together earlier. Those already in the sauna stayed.

"Somebody feed me." John Cangelose bobbed up from the water. Corrie carried a tuna salad sandwich to him and held it over the pool's edge for him to take a bite. Somebody called him a porpoise. He answered that he was a porpoise with a purpose.

Eventually, we all clustered into little groups in the heated sauna or wrapped in towels around the pool. Several times, Tina had to tell everybody to keep the noise level to a minimal roar, since arrangements with the manager had been tenuous, at best.

A car with very bright lights pulled into a parking space directly outside the fence surrounding the pool. Coach Charba got out and came over to where I was sitting and congratulated me. She only stayed a few minutes, but I thought it was nice of her to drop by.

When she backed out, Rob drove up. I tried to continue my conversation with Corrie about those from other schools who'd been picked for All-State. We'd been recalling names and trying to match faces from teams we'd played.

Tim Lacey, in the pool, grabbed Rob's ankle as he walked by and tried to pull him in. "Where's your suit, or do you plan to swim in that?"

"Neither." He pulled free and kept walking toward me.

"You're late," I said to him. "Did you have to make all the rounds first?" I meant it as a joke.

"No, I didn't," he answered. His low-keyed tone didn't match mine. "I . . . I just had to do a little thinking first." He pulled a lounge chair closer to where I sat, and Corrie excused herself and left us alone.

"Congratulations," he said. His tone was definitely different, but I couldn't quite put my finger on the change.

"Thanks."

There was a long silence. I couldn't think of a single witty thing to say. "This was really a surprise," I finally got out.

Rob looked around at John Cangelose, neck above the water, chattering his teeth together in perfect rhythm.

I nodded toward the table of food. "You want something?"

"No, I just want to talk to you." He looked around over his shoulder. "Okay? Or do you have a date with Jared?"

"No, I don't have a date with Jared. Tina didn't catch him at home." I couldn't help my exasperated tone; surely, he'd gotten the message by now. Jared was just a friend! How many different ways did I have to say it?

"Can we talk someplace else? How about if we drive somewhere?"

I thought it over. "I don't think so. The party's in my honor. I don't think it'd be too courteous to walk out in the middle of it."

"Guess you're right," he answered. Then he pulled his chair around to face me. I scooted back in my own chair and sat waiting for him to say something. After a moment, he stood up, gently lifted my feet over the side of the lounger, and sat down on the edge next to them. He looked at me for a long time, still saying nothing. Then he said, "You're stubborn, you know that?"

"I've been told that a few times," I smiled. "But I've never believed a word of it."

He took my hand.

"You never did say why you were late. Cheerleading celebrations?"

"There were, but I didn't go."

I raised my eyebrows and waited, but he didn't explain. His blue eyes danced at me. Finally, he said, "You have no mercy, lady, do you? You want me to get down and crawl?" He dropped off the side of the chair onto all fours, lowered his head, and nipped at the calf of my leg.

I couldn't help but laugh, and I started pushing at him to make him stop. Everybody was looking at us. Then he caught my ankle when I stood up to escape. With one sudden twist, I flipped right into the swimming pool, headfirst. When I came up spewing water, he held out a hand to me. I couldn't decide whether to take it and pull myself out or grab his wrist and pull him in, clothes and all.

Just then, Tina's mother came to the top of the stairs and hollered down that there was a phone call for me. I wrapped the towel around my soggy suit and traipsed lightly over her living room carpet.

"Leanne?" It was Jared. He sounded far away, and there was so much loud music in the background that I could hardly hear him.

"Yeah, it's me. Where are you?"

"I just wanted to say good-bye."

"Jared, where are you?"

"At home, now. But I'm leaving—for good."

"Why?"

"I . . . I don't want to talk about it now. I'll write."

"Write me from where?"

"I don't know yet."

"Jared. . . ."

"Look, I didn't mean to interrupt anything. When I called you at home, your mother gave me Tina's number."

"It's okay. You didn't interrupt anything." I thought about Rob

"It's okay. You didn't interrupt anything." I thought about Rob still standing by the pool waiting for me and the fact that we'd finally seemed to get together.

"I just wanted to say good-bye. We didn't talk much when you came over yesterday afternoon."

"Yeah. Well, it had nothing to do with you. It was a ballot problem."

"A what?"

"Nothing. I'm over that, anyway. Listen, what's happened?"

He sounded unemotional, detached. "I've got to get away from my dad."

"But where will you go?"

"I don't know. I'll decide that by the time I get to the ticket counter."

"Then tell me why. What did he do?"

I could hear him swallow hard several times, but he didn't say anything for a minute.

"Look," I said, "just wait. I'll be right over. Wait for me."

"No. Don't. I didn't call for that. I just wanted to say thanks. You're the best friend I've ever had." He sounded alone, weak, tired, and scared.

"Jared, wait for me. I'm coming over." I hung up and went into Tina's bedroom to dress.

chapter sixteen

As I walked up to Jared's front door, I tried to fluff up my wet hair. I'd driven the car with the window down, although I knew better than to be out alone after dark in an unlocked car. I thought about Rob waiting for me out by the pool and knew I should have gone back to explain, rather than just vanish.

But remembering what he'd said the day in the park about my running to Jared whenever he snapped his fingers, I couldn't have gone back out to face him. If he couldn't understand—well, he just couldn't understand. I didn't have time to worry about it.

I could hear Mr. Sahol's voice and a woman's laughter, and loud music blaring out in the back around the pool, but I rang the front doorbell. My insides quivered, and I didn't know if it was from the damp hair and chill or the thought that my coming was an intrusion on Mr. Sahol's privacy. Maybe this was family business Jared didn't even want to discuss with me. But I remembered his mother and how he'd needed me then. And during my parents' divorce, I'd certainly wanted Jared with me then. After two more rings of the bell, I decided I'd have to walk around to the back before somebody would hear me. If he hadn't waited. . . .

Through the open back gate, I saw Mr. Sahol in his swim trunks, with a Hawaiian shirt fluttering open to the waist. He swaggered over and picked up a drink off the patio table. As I got further around the driveway, Jared and Carmen came into view. In her bikini, she had draped herself across a lounger and faced Mr. Sahol with provocatively pouting lips. Jared was the only one fully dressed. He was holding a duffel bag in his hand.

I panicked. In light of Mr. Sahol's tendency to make snap assumptions, seeing me at this very moment, he might think Jared and I planned to leave the country together. But it was too late to turn around. They all saw me on the driveway at the corner of the house at the same time.

"Well, Leanne. Leanne!" Mr. Sahol waved his glass in my direction. "Come in and see if you can make out what this little discussion is all about."

I walked a few steps further in their direction, but I wasn't about to try to explain any discussion to anybody.

Red-faced, Jared yelled, "You just leave her out of this!"

I stood frozen where I was in the driveway.

"What's that?" His dad let out a satirical snort and chuckle. "Surely, you never thought you were man enough to keep her, either, did you? How about it, Leanne? He tells me you two broke up. Not that I blame you any." He lifted his glass toward me in a mock toast.

"I said leave her out of this!"

"Listen to this, Carmen," his dad continued, after gulping another swallow. "Sit up and just listen to this, would you? We've got a real little man speaking up now."

I glanced at Carmen. She wore the same bemused expression she'd had on at my party.

Mr. Sahol continued. "Leanne, isn't he cute? Too bad it's past his bedtime."

"Shut up! Shut up!" Jared, screaming and crying at the same time, lunged for his dad. Mr. Sahol tried to sidestep him, but Jared caught his arm and the wine glass shattered as it banged down on the patio table. Blood started running in little rivulets from Mr. Sahol's arm.

"Stop it! Just stop it!" I yelled at both of them. They ignored me as they clutched at each other, pushing forward, then backward at the edge of the pool. Carmen grabbed her towel and finally sat up, holding her hand over her mouth, her eyes wide.

"Let me go." Jared gave him one last shove and wrenched himself loose from his dad's drunken, slippery grasp. "Just let me go."

Mr. Sahol started after him, stepped on a chunk of glass, caught his foot in pain, and then lost his balance, hitting his head on the side of the pool as his body plunged under the water.

We waited. And waited. All three of us converged at the side of the pool where he'd slipped into the water. The ripples grew smaller and wider. We waited.

"Jared, he's not coming up!" I screamed. "He's not coming up!" We could see his dad's figure slumped at the bottom of the deep end about four or five feet away from the pool's edge.

Jared yanked off his shoes and dove in. After what seemed like an eternity, he reappeared on the water's surface, dragging his father under his arm. Carmen and I both helped lift him out onto the tile beside the pool. Jared slapped him and then pressed his chest like I'd seen them do on TV. After what seemed like forever, his dad opened his eyes and started coughing and spewing out water.

Through the whole thing, Carmen kept muttering, "Are you all right? Is he going to be all right? Are you all right, Dennis? Is he going to be all right?"

How did I know? I grabbed his cut hand and arm and started to wrap them tightly in a beach towel. As I finished, Mr. Sahol rolled himself over on his side and finally sat up.

"Are you all right? Are you going to be all right?" Carmen kept up the litany, her big, round, doe eyes about two inches from his face.

He turned away from her and sat up. "Yeah. I'm going to be all right."

"What do you want me to do?" she whimpered again. "Call the doctor?"

"No."

"Mr. Sahol, I think you really should get to a doctor," I cut in. "You're going to have to have stitches."

He started to cry. Whether from the pain or the alcohol or what, I couldn't tell. It scared me.

Carmen bent down to his face again.

Wearily and blubbering, he said to her, "Get my car keys and just go home."

"Don't you want me to. . . ."

"Just get your things and go home!" He kept shaking his head, sobbing. Carmen backed away and darted off through the house like a frightened fawn.

I stuck my head in the doorway after her and shouted into the dark house. "Jared, come on. Hurry! We've got to take your dad to a hospital."

No answer.

"Jared?"

Still no answer. I ran back around to the driveway. Jared's car was gone; so was the duffel bag he'd dropped on the patio earlier. There I was, left with a bleeding man I had come to loathe in the last few minutes.

So what to do? Take Mr. Sahol to the hospital emergency room, or go after Jared? Jared had said he'd decide where he was going when he got to the ticket counter. I assumed he'd meant that he planned to fly.

Indecisively, I made my way back to Mr. Sahol, who had stopped sobbing, but was still sitting on the tile holding the towel around his arm. "Where's Jared?" He looked up at me.

"I don't know, but we need to catch him. He was headed for the airport, I think."

He didn't clarify or contradict my assumptions. He only began to sob again, louder this time. My heart pounded. I'd never seen a grown man cry. One minute, he was a boisterous, insulting drunk and the next, he was sobbing like a baby. But what about Jared? What if he got on that plane? What if he never called home again? What if. . . .

I touched his shoulder. "Mr. Sahol, listen to me. Do you think I should go after Jared? Or do I need to get you to the emergency room?" My heart still pounded, and my mind pulled me in both directions.

He muttered something through his folded arms.

"Mr. Sahol, we need to catch Jared. And you need to get to the hospital—you're still bleeding." I wondered if I sounded more assertive than I felt. Where was Mother? I should call her to come help, but where had she and Philip gone for the evening?

"Mr. Sahol?" I pulled his arm toward me and tightened the towel.

He looked up at me. "He pulled me out. He wouldn't have pulled me out if he hated me, would he? It's my fault."

"No, he doesn't hate you, Mr. Sahol," I said, my voice shaking. "But can we go to the airport? If he gets on a plane and we don't know where he's going, with the way he's feeling now. . . ."

Mr. Sahol, to my surprise, got to his feet and followed me to my car. We headed for the airport.

"Which airline?" I wondered aloud.

"They're all in the same terminal. He'll try to get on the first plane that leaves."

I drove in silence, not asking Mr. Sahol what any of this had been about. What had happened in the last two weeks that was so bad Jared hadn't even returned my phone calls? But as he sat dejectedly and very soberly beside me, I wanted to understand this man. What would make a father treat his son the way he'd begun to treat Jared in the last few months? I didn't want to hate him, anymore than I had wanted to hate Kathi. Nevertheless, the lump of hardness was still there, clogging my mind and my sympathy.

"I never meant to hurt him with Carmen," he blubbered. "I swear I didn't. She didn't mean anything, anyway. None of them ever did. Jared's wrong."

I cleared my throat, thinking I wasn't old enough to hear any of this.

"Your party was the start of it all."

Wrong. He was dead wrong. He'd been putting Jared down for a lot longer than the two weeks since my party. I remembered his comment on the phone extension, and his look of scorn when I had said I couldn't stay for dinner that evening when he'd brought home another twenty-year-old. And all the other comments he'd made about how Jared should buy a few friends.

I swallowed again, not wanting to hear the details and wanting to hear them, all the same. I glanced at him out of the corner of my eye. Did he really know what he was saying now? Was he sober?

He seemed oblivious to my discomfort at his confessions. He continued, "He brought her back by the house that night, to listen to records. And I came downstairs because I'd met her at the club the night before. She just kept leading me on. You can understand that, can't you?"

I cleared my throat noiselessly, trying not to breathe too loudly. But I didn't answer him one way or the other.

"And when he offered to take her home, she said she wasn't ready to go yet. He just gave up and went upstairs. His mother was sick so long. I drove her home later."

I wasn't sure if I knew what he meant, but I didn't want to know more. We were not too far from the airport.

"If she hadn't gotten sick. . . ."

I nodded at him vaguely and kept my eyes on the road.

"Have you ever seen what cancer does to you? Day after day she was in agony." He started sobbing again. "I couldn't—I just couldn't—stand to see her suffer."

I knew what he meant. It had been Mary, Jared and I who'd helped her sip broth through a straw. We sat noiselessly around her bed and heard her breathing grow lighter and lighter, and we'd seen her face contort when the medication began to wear off. I knew.

"He thought I didn't love her. But I did. I did! I'll never get over her. Life'll never be the same again."

He started to sob again. My eyes filled, too, and I thought we never would get to the airport. But as I finally pulled a parking ticket from the meter box and the wooden arm lifted to admit us, I tried to pull it all together. So this was what Jared had building inside him since his mother's death and his dad's frenzied dating began. He'd probably been vacillating between anger at his dad for his behavior with Carmen and loathing for himself at letting his dad make him feel inadequate as a man. It didn't matter that Jared wasn't interested in Carmen personally; it was just the idea of the whole thing. I could understand why he hadn't called me. He wasn't ready to talk to anyone about still another failure.

Just as we entered the terminal, Mr. Sahol, still holding the bloody towel around his arm, spotted Jared. He stood in line at the Delta counter.

Mr. Sahol headed in Jared's direction, but I hung back. The terminal was small enough that I wouldn't lose sight of them. This was something they had to get straight on their own. Jared had saved his father's life before he'd walked out; surely there was enough feeling left to rebuild their relationship, if they both wanted to try.

I watched as Mr. Sahol touched Jared on the shoulder and pulled him around into his arms.

* * *

It was almost midnight when I got back to my car. I'd phoned Mother from the airport to tell her where I was, promising to wake her and explain everything when I came in. There was no use going back to Tina's apartment; everybody would be gone by the time I got there. Particularly Rob. A phone call in the morning would set things right with Tina.

I tried to imagine what she'd said to Rob. No matter what she'd come up with, it would all have finally crystallized to the same point: Jared was still in the picture. Rob had said that I had no mercy. Of course, I knew he had been teasing, but my disappearing act to see Jared would be too much, even if Rob had been on the verge of swallowing a little pride.

On the way to the hospital, where I dropped Mr. Sahol and Jared to get stitches, and then home, I went over in my mind everything Jared had said, the look in his face while he was talking. He'd be okay. He'd been through a lot before with his mother's death and now his father's indiscretion, but he'd make it. Both of them would.

Neither Matt Corley nor I would leave them alone until they had worked things out right. That was the difference, I decided. With boyfriends, you had to stay in close touch to keep the flame going. But friends were forever.

When I turned down our street, Rob's Honda was parked in my driveway. After the initial shock, I panicked. My emotional circuits were already near overload. Two confrontations in one night were more than I could handle.

"Have a seat," he called to me through his lowered window as he pushed open the door on my side. I got out of my car and slid into his. We didn't say anything for a minute. "Tina said you had an emergency."

"Yeah, kind of." I couldn't decide if he knew it was about Jared or not. "I didn't expect you to be here," I said.

"I didn't expect me to be here, either." His eyes danced at me in the moonlight. "I left the party when you did, and I've been thinking. I guess what I want to say is that I'm ready to stand in line."

His eyes searched my face while he rubbed the back of my neck with his thumb and forefinger.

"What do you mean?"

"Stand in line," he repeated. "You know, take my chances along with the rest. Jared, or whoever."

"But you don't have to. . . ."

Before I could finish, he added, "You remember what I said the first night we dated and then that Sunday afternoon in the park? About not wanting someone who was interested in someone else?"

I nodded.

"I've been thinking that I haven't been quite fair. Just because I spend a lot of time on the golf course and have my dream woman picked out, that doesn't mean you've done the same about me."

"Rob, it's not that. . . ."

"No," he raised his hand to shush me, "let me finish. I got to thinking about what Tina said tonight on the phone. I was giving her some line about how I planned to make some other parties tonight. Put in an appearance for the council and all that rot. She thought I was stupid."

"I don't think she thought. . . ."

"Yes, she did." He cut me off again. "Would you be quiet for a minute and let me finish? I don't apologize too often. You might even want to get this on tape, because I might deny I said it tomorrow."

I smiled at him. He was gorgeous.

"What I'm saying is that I've had more time to make up my mind about you than you've had to make up your mind about me. Subpart B of Subpart II, as my lawyer dad would say, is: If you're not going out with Jared tomorrow night, could we go to dinner and a movie, or something?"

"I'd love to."

Then he leaned over and kissed me. His kiss was twice as good as I remembered. We sat there a few minutes longer, staring at each other.

Finally he said, "You want to tell me about the emergency?"

I told him about Jared, but not all the details. When I finished, he said, "I guess I should be embarrassed for putting him down before. Sounds like he's been through a lot of junk."

"It's okay. You didn't know."

"You think he'll be all right?"

I nodded.

"I guess he needed someone like you, to help him handle it all."

"I wasn't much help yesterday when I was over there. I knew he was upset about something, but I was so wrapped up in myself, I didn't even ask about him."

"What are you smiling about?" he asked.

"It's not over till it's over."

"What's that supposed to mean?"

"A rough biblical translation."

He shrugged, still puzzled.

"I'll explain later. Sometime when we can start the discussion before midnight."

Rob looked pensive and kept running his left hand around the steering wheel. "It's hard for me to understand what a guy like that goes through, you know? I've got both my parents, and they're great. I guess I've got everything."

The light flashed on and off inside the house a couple of times. "So have I," I said, nodding toward the light. "My mother wants *me* to know that *she* knows that *I* know it's time to come in."

He opened the door, and I slid out on his side. "About tomorrow night. Where would you like to eat?"

"Not a poolside restaurant, for sure."

He kissed the tip of my nose. "Yeah, I agree. You owe me one good dunk, don't you?"

"Never fear, I'll be at your next diving meet."

"Not on your life! An audience makes me nervous."

I hooted at that. "Rob Cantrell, you've never been nervous in your life."

We were on the front steps by then. I turned around to tell him good night. He kissed me again very lightly and walked back toward his car. Before I got inside, he called to me. "If Jared calls you—I guess he will, won't he?—tell him . . . if you think it's appropriate and all . . . that I'm sorry about his dad and . . . everything."

"Sure," I said. I closed the front door behind me and leaned against it for a moment. Given a little time, Rob and I could become really good friends.

For Further Reflection

---

1. What were Leanne's strengths and weaknesses as a new Christian?
2. How do you define loyalty?
3. How was her feeling of responsibility toward Jared a test of her faith?
4. What do you think of Rob's position about Jared and Leanne's relationship? Why?
5. Where do you think responsibility for a friend should end?
6. Why was Leanne angry with herself about the way she reacted to the balloting situation? How had she "failed" Tina's and her own mother's expectations? In what way had she met her mother's expectations, perhaps without realizing it?
7. Can you point out some evidences of Leanne's influence on Jared?
8. What did you think was the turning point in Rob and Leanne's relationship?
9. What scriptural verses and principles could have guided Leanne in her moments of decision?
10. Have you ever felt responsible for a friend? If so, how did you handle the situation?
11. What are some ways to mediate between your friends who may not get along?